A Catalina Cove Christmas

LOVE, PASSION AND PROMISE BOOKS
are published by
The Madaris Publishing Company
P O Box 28267
Jacksonville, FL 32226

ISBN 978-0-9799165-9-5
0-9799165-9-3

10 9 8 7 6 5 4 3 2 1
Printed in the United States of America

A
Catalina Cove
Christmas

BRENDA JACKSON

Love, Passion and Promise
An Imprint of the
Madaris Publishing Company

www.madarispublishing.com

Dear Readers,

When I began the three-book Catalina Cove Series, I was testing the waters to see how you would like a series that was not family related but where the town itself was the main character. I introduced you to the fictional town of Catalina Cove, Louisiana. I wanted you to get to know some of the cove's residences, and not a particular family.

Because Catalina Cove is a small shipping town, a stone's throw away from New Orleans, most of the people know each other and have been friends for years – so there will be friends who attended the same schools. However, because it is an attractive town, new people are moving in. Then there are those who'd moved away for college are moving back. I am excited about the people I want you to meet.

One such person is Isaac Elloran. I introduced Isaac in Book 2, Forget Me Not, and told you more about him in Book 3, Finding Home Again. He was born and raised in Catalina Cove, but left for college. Now he's back and has a story to tell. Isaac is divorced and his ex-wife, Donna, was also his high school sweetheart. I love high school sweethearts' stories!

There is a high school homecoming planned in Catalina Cove around Christmas. Both Isaac and Donna will be attending. Can they use this holiday occasion to heal old wounds, get to know each other again, and decide if they still want a future together?

I hope you enjoy reading Isaac and Donna's story where it is once again proven that true love conquers all.

Happy Holidays!

Brenda Jackson

DEDICATION

To the man who will always be the love of my life, Gerald Jackson, Sr. My first. My last. My everything.

To everyone who requested a visit to Catalina Cove during Christmas time, this book is for you.

To all my readers everywhere, I wish you the best this Holiday Season!

There is an appointed time for everything. And there is a time for every event under heaven. Ecclesiastes 3:1 (NIV)

BOOKS IN THE CATALINA COVE SERIES BY BRENDA JACKSON

Love in Catalina Cove
Forget Me Not
Finding Home Again
A Catalina Cove Christmas
Follow Your Heart -coming October 2020

Chapter One

Isaac Elloran was awakened at three in the morning to the sounds of a wolf howling—a wolf in Catalina Cove, Louisiana of all places. He knew the sound was coming from Acer, the pet wolf that belonged to his neighbor's son Tyler. No one figured the little pup the Lassiter's had found hungry and abandoned six months ago during a camping trip to the Smokey Mountains would grow up to howl at the moon.

Usually Acer's calls wouldn't bother Isaac—he was used to sleeping right through them. But not tonight. And it wasn't just because of Acer. His mind was still racing after the conversation he'd had with Kaegan Chambray earlier that day. Kaegan owned a local seafood shipping company. After an arson-related fire on one of his boats last month, Kaegan had hired him to install security cameras around the docks where the boats were located.

Kaegan, who was on the Catalina Cove High School's holiday homecoming planning committee, had mentioned the invitations to the event had been mailed. They were expecting a lot of people to return to the cove for the reunion.

Isaac couldn't help wondering if Donna Oliver Elloran, his ex-wife, would come. It had been nearly three years since their divorce. He sometimes thought he'd managed to get over her but knew he was just fooling himself. The incentive to move on wasn't there and wondered if it ever would be.

And that was the crux of his problem.

He should hate her for what she did to them—choosing her career over him and their marriage. But as much as he wanted to, he couldn't. Right now, he just didn't like her very much. She'd made returning to Catalina Cove, the place he'd always loved and considered home, difficult. Everyone had wanted to know what could have possibly happened for him and Donna to end their marriage. They'd not only been the darlings of their high school, but they'd been the darlings of Catalina Cove as well. They'd been expected to be the couple who would live out their lives in Catalina Cove, celebrating their seventy-fifth wedding anniversary with their kids, grands and great-grands. It was a cruel twist of fate that such a thing wouldn't be happening.

Easing out of bed, he left his bedroom to go into the kitchen to get a beer out the refrigerator, not caring about the time. Time was something he had a lot of these days. After making millions on the company he'd sold last year, he'd been fortunate to be able to retire at thirty-three. He doubted Donna knew that. He also doubted that she knew he had left Boston to move back to Catalina Cove, the place the two of them had been born, raised, and schooled, before leaving for college in Seattle.

After living in the dorms for two years, they'd moved off campus into an apartment. Six months after graduating from the University of Seattle, they'd gotten married. The newlyweds had been lucky to get hired by top companies within their chosen field. Isaac had an engineering technology degree and Donna, a degree in advertising and public relations. Then, after they'd been married for two years, Isaac had decided to go back to school part-time for his MBA.

He and Donna had always been a team; as a couple they'd made all their decisions together. One of those decisions was to wait to have children until after they'd kick-started their careers. They'd hoped that after sending their kids to college, they'd be able to retire in Catalina Cove one day. They both loved the small town where they'd grown up.

Everything had been going good for them, but he hadn't counted on a few things happening—things that had driven a wedge between them; things that had destroyed the very essence of their lives together.

Not wanting to dwell on the bad times between him and his ex-wife, he forced his mind to remember happier ones. Way back to the beginning, when he and Donna had realized they wanted more than just friendship.

Leaving the kitchen, Isaac went to the family room where the fire he'd started in the fireplace earlier that evening was still blazing, bringing heat to the lower part of the house. He headed to the bookcase where he kept the one book he and Donna would thumb through while cuddled on the sofa, whenever they got homesick. They'd reminisce about the past and think about old friends, wondering where they were now and what they were doing. Had they reached their dreams and were they as happy as he and Donna were?

Pulling down his yearbook, he moved to the sofa with his beer. He wasn't sure who appeared most in the yearbook, him or Donna. She'd been popular, well-liked by all. He'd been captain of the football, basketball, track, and swim teams, as well as the president of the school's technology team, bringing home trophies from several computer science fairs every year. Needless to say, he hadn't been a typical geek—he'd proven a guy could be a good athlete as well as a techy. He'd been as obsessed with computers as much as he'd been with sports—but he'd been obsessed with Donna more than either of them.

Opening the yearbook, he immediately went to the section where he knew a number of Donna's photos were located. In one picture, she was smiling bright for the camera in her cheerleader outfit. He thought the same thing now that he'd thought then—Donna Marie Oliver was beautiful. Her hair was curly and long, spilling over her shoulders, and cascading around her oval face. Her eyes were dark and expressive; her cheekbones high and her mouth still looked deliciously sweet.

However, it was her long legs he liked seeing the most. They were shapely and gorgeous and always looked great in those short skirts she wore. Underneath the photos listed all her activities, which even then had been impressive.

He flipped to the section where his photo was located. He had a list of activities underneath his picture, as well. Both he and Donna had been voted "Most Likely to Succeed". Donna had also been voted "Most Popular Girl" and he'd been chosen as "Most Popular Guy".

As he continued to flip the pages, his mind drifted back to when he'd thought the love, the romance and passion, would last forever.

The passion...

That was one thing he didn't want to think about right now. He missed it more than anything. It had never waned between them, even when their relationship began unraveling. Make-up sex had always rocked both their worlds.

He forced his mind back in focus and finished going through the yearbook, remembering when his life had pretty much been close to perfect.

Or so he'd thought.

Six years earlier

"Congratulations sweetheart," Isaac said, clinking his champagne glass against his wife's.

"And congratulations to you, too," Donna said, smiling over at him.

Isaac returned her smile as they sipped their champagne. He'd made reservations at what had become their favorite restaurant in downtown Seattle. Tonight, they both had something to celebrate—Donna's promotion at work to Advertising Manager, and Isaac's letter from the University of Seattle, stating that he'd completed all the requirements for his MBA and would be graduating in the spring.

"Now I'll have more time to spend with you. I appreciate you putting up with my schedule the last three years," he said.

"You would have done the same for me, Isaac. We're a team, remember."

Yes, he remembered and was grateful for it. He'd dreamed about getting his MBA for years. It hadn't been easy. He'd continued working full-time at Meyers Technology and attended classes at night, which often meant leaving work going straight to class, and spending weekends, studying. It had taken him three years to complete, but Donna had been behind him all the way. He couldn't have done it without her.

Before long, the waitress brought their meal and over dinner, Donna told him what her new duties would entail. He lifted his head at something she said. "Traveling?"

She smiled over at him. "Not much, but yes. I'm happy about it."

He heard the excitement in her voice. She'd always liked traveling and he figured that with an airline pilot for a father, and a former flight attendant as a mother, it was in her blood. The Olivers were known to leave the cove at the beginning of every summer and not return until just weeks before the beginning of school in the fall. Donna would tell everyone about all the cool places they'd visited, both in the U.S. and abroad.

Isaac's father had owned a repair shop in town; and he fixed anything and everything—from appliances to televisions to computers. He'd been an only child and his mother had died when he'd been ten. Because his father worked long hours at his repair shop, there hadn't been time or money for travelling, other than the hour-long drive they would sometime take to spend a day in New Orleans. That was the only travelling he'd ever done as a kid.

Even now, he rarely traveled with his job and when he did, he was anxious to get home. He disliked being away from Donna for long periods of time. He preferred to have her close to him every night, snuggled up beside him in their big bed. Just thinking of her going on business trips had him missing her already.

"Anything else about this promotion that I need to know?"

He'd tried keeping the sting from his voice but knew she'd heard it when she lifted a brow. "It's no different than any of your promotions, Isaac. I will be in training for a few weeks, which means I will probably bring reading material home, like you did on occasion."

His wife was typically easygoing, calm, and laid-back. However, if she felt the need to set him straight about anything, she had no problem doing it—albeit in a nice, but to-the-point sort of way. Donna could hold her own against anyone, including him.

Knowing when to back off, he reached out and took her hand in his. "Just let me know what I can do to make things easier for you, sweetheart. I have your back."

The smile that spread across her face at that moment was one he'd remember forever. And if it was possible, it made him fall even more in love with her. "Thanks, Isaac."

"For you Donna, always."

Chapter Two

"You're doing a great job, Donna. You're becoming a real asset to the company."

"Thank you, Mr. Chase."

A huge smile spread across Donna's lips when her boss walked out of her office. It was good to be appreciated. Especially since she'd given the Belcher project everything she had.

It was hard to believe that it had been a year since she'd become an Advertising Manager. During that time, she'd worked on a number of accounts, but she'd known the Belcher account was the biggest—Belcher Department Store was one of the company's most important clients.

Others in the office had been surprised she'd managed to land such an important account, which spoke volumes of Mr. Chase's faith in her abilities. Of course, over the past year, she'd gone above and beyond, working late and coming into the office on the weekends. But with achievements came sacrifices. And unfortunately, one of those sacrifices had been time with Isaac. But she hadn't had much choice—not if she wanted to succeed in her career.

Initially, Isaac had been understanding and supportive. He still was, but to a lesser degree now and in a way, that annoyed her. She'd told him in the beginning about the traveling she would have to do. Granted, it had ended up being more than she'd thought. However, she made it a point to call Isaac every night from her hotel room, needing to hear his voice before drifting off to sleep.

He would tell her how his day had gone, and she would talk about hers. Then they would say how much they missed each other, and how much they loved each other before ending the call. But she'd known nothing could replace sharing the same bed at night, making love before going to sleep, and being held in his arms during the night. But she loved her job, and was hoping to make

Advertising Director in a few years. Why couldn't he understand that?

It could be because his promotion six months ago hadn't had the life-altering effect on their marriage that hers had. He did travel, but only once in a blue moon. And regardless of his demands at work, he always made her his priority. She'd tried to do the same for him but there had been times when she'd failed. She knew that.

She remembered bailing on one of his important office parties because she'd needed to work. And another time, she'd cancelled their much-anticipated vacation to the mountains when Mr. Chase had dropped another important project on her desk at the last minute.

Okay, she would admit that lately, she hadn't been the best wife in the world. But hopefully, with a number of her accounts finished and out the way, she'd be able to slow things down a bit. She smiled when an idea popped into her head. Picking up the phone, she called Isaac.

"I hope you're calling because you want me, sweetheart."

She chuckled, knowing she would always want him. "The big question is, do you want me, Isaac?"

She wondered why she would ask such a thing. Her husband always wanted her. Isaac had no trouble letting her know how desirable he found her. Unfortunately, with her loaded schedule, lately she'd deliberately ignored Isaac's I-want-you signs a few times.

"I'll always want you, Donna."

She leaned back in her chair. "Then how about meeting your wife for lunch."

"Where?"

"At the home of Isaac and Donna Elloran. Need the address?"

A delicious shudder rushed through her body at the sound of his chuckle. "No, I think I'll be able to find it."

"Make sure you do. Be there in thirty-minutes. I'll pick up lunch. And just so you know, I'm taking the rest of the day off."

She could imagine the shocked look on his face. She hadn't taken any time off work, not even as much as an hour, since getting her promotion a year ago. She'd been practically working non-stop.

"In that case, I'll take the afternoon off as well."

She could hear the sound of his keys, which meant he was already leaving his office. "See you in a few, Isaac."

"I'm on my way."

When he clicked off the phone, she drew in a deep breath knowing she'd never been able to do that for him...drop her work at the spur of the moment and leave the office. Maybe starting today, she'd change her way of thinking. She needed to remember who was the most important person in her life.

For the past year, she'd put her work before her husband but that was about to change.

Isaac pulled into the driveway. Donna's car was already parked there. When was the last time that happened? Usually, it meant she was inside packing for one of her trips. She'd had plenty of those—unexpected ones where her boss had informed her at the last minute that she needed to go heaven knows where. Of course, she would drop everything, including Isaac, and go.

Opening the door and entering the house, he went into the kitchen and saw the bags on the table from his favorite sandwich shop. He left the kitchen and glanced around. Then he saw her jacket on the floor. He lifted a brow as he picked it up. His wife was one of the tidiest people he knew. She would never drop her jacket on the floor and leave it there.

Then he saw her skirt, lying a few feet away from her jacket. Moving forward, he picked it up as well. He smiled when he realized what *she'd* done—and what she expected *him* to do. Follow the trail.

He moved toward the stairs and upon reaching the landing, he glanced down and saw her bra and panties. There was no need to call out for her since he knew exactly where she would be.

The double doors to their bedroom were closed but he knew she was in there. The chiming of the door when he'd entered the house had to have alerted her to his entrance. That meant...she was waiting for him.

Not wanting to keep her waiting, he loosened his tie before opening the door. He immediately saw her, lying on top of the bedcovers, naked. Their gazes met and held for a long moment before she eased up in the bed, giving him a delectable frontal view. "I thought you would never get here."

He didn't bother closing the door behind him. They were in their house, in their bedroom. "I'm here now, sweetheart," he said, kicking off his shoes and bending over to remove his socks.

"Good."

She watched intently as he stripped off every stitch of clothing that he'd worn to work that day. When he was completely naked, he moved toward the bed, toward her. "Just so you know, Donna, on the way home I made a mental list of all the things I wanted to do to you when I got here."

Her smile widened. "Should I be scared?"

He shook his head. "No. Just be ready to get worn out."

She leaned up and wrapped her arms around his neck. "I could suggest the same thing for you." Then she pressed her mouth to his.

He let her, hoping he'd survive this Donna Elloran kiss—the kind of kiss he'd taught her he liked, and that she'd perfected over the years. Suddenly, he was completely devoid of logical thought. The only thing on his mind was taking things to another level with his wife. Although they had the rest of the day to do this, he'd arrived already aroused, anticipating just what he would be getting when he got home. And his wife wasn't disappointing him.

She suddenly pulled back and whispered against his lips. "I want to taste you."

Was she serious? Donna knew he wouldn't be able to last if she put her mouth on him. "I don't think that's a good idea, sweetheart. I need to get inside of you bad."

"Umm, that's what you always say."

"And that's what I always mean, Donna."

Before giving her a chance to protest, he quickly eased her down in bed on her back. Now he had her just where he wanted her. Beneath him. She'd have a chance to taste him later, the same way he intended to do with her. He glanced down at her and almost drowned in those pitch-black eyes staring back at him.

Total awareness had taken over his senses the moment he'd picked her clothing off the floor. Now, he was not only totally aware but also fully charged. He recognized that look. It was one that warned him that here, in their bedroom, was not a place for sin, shock, or shame. The sky was the limit and she intended for them to fly high today.

For a brief moment, he wondered if she was preparing him for something? Another promotion at work that required even more traveling, perhaps? She must have detected his worry and said, "Today is about you and me, Isaac. Nothing else. Are you ready to be exhausted?"

Hell yes, he was ready. "More than ready. But I have a question for you."

"And what is that?" she asked him.

The sound of her voice had need burning into his brain. He shifted, his thighs touching her and immediately blood throbbed in his veins. "Knowing how horny I can get, are you sure you can handle me? It's been a while."

She reached up and wrapped her arms around his neck. "I have hours to try, right?"

"Right."

"Then let's get it on, Isaac Elloran."

Chapter Three

D onna Elloran pulled into the parking lot of her favorite spa. Finally, she would get the day of beauty she deserved. Glancing around, she noticed all the holiday decorations and felt pain ripple through her. She could usually deal with the loneliness, but this time of the year was especially hard. Being a thirty-four-year-old divorced woman was the pits.

She turned off the ignition, unbuckled her seat belt, and was about to open the car door and go inside the building when her phone rang. Digging it out of her purse, from the ringtone she knew that it was her best friend from high school, Nina Murray. Smiling, she clicked on the phone. "Hey Nina, what's up?"

"Are you going?" Nina asked in an excited voice.

Donna lifted a brow. "Going where?"

"Honestly Donna, when was the last time you checked your mail?"

Donna glanced at her watch. She'd arrived at the spa with ten minutes to spare. "Umm, who wants to know?"

"I do. If you checked your mail on a regular basis like most people, you would have found an invitation. If I got one, then I'm sure the most popular girl at Catalina Cove High School got one as well."

Donna looked perplexed. "What are you talking about?"

"What I'm talking about is that the six graduating classes that had Mr. Harding as principal are getting together for a homecoming. But it's not just any homecoming—it's a holiday homecoming. So, are you going to go?"

Without even thinking, Donna said, "I don't think so. Chances are the most popular boy at Catalina Cove High School will be there as well."

"So what? At least you two did what everyone figured you would do—get married," Nina said. "However, I will admit, I'm certain nobody counted on the divorce."

Donna knew it was time to change the subject, or at least try to. It wasn't always easy with Nina. "Where are you?"

"On my way to the store. I had a long, tiring day at the hospital. Three extra hours. So, I went home first to take a nap."

"Long, tiring days for you are the norm," Donna said. Nina worked as a trauma nurse at a hospital in Los Angeles.

"Look who's talking. I remember when you were the overtime queen. One who didn't know when to go home."

That's the last thing Donna wanted to remember. Deciding to make another attempt to change the subject, she said. "Are you in the Christmas spirit yet?" She already knew the answer. Nina loved the holidays and usually had decorations up the first week in November, bypassing Thanksgiving altogether. Nina never operated by anyone's holiday timeline but her own.

"Of course, I am. I put up my Christmas tree over the weekend. That's why I'm on my way to the store. I need to buy more lights, since most of the ones from last year don't work. What about you? Have you gotten a tree yet?"

"No."

"You didn't get one last year or the year before that, Donna."

"And I don't intend to get one this year either." Donna glanced at her watch again. "Look Nina, I need to run. My spa appointment is in less than five minutes and Jean is a stickler for punctuality."

"Okay, but please consider going to the holiday homecoming. You know how long I've been looking forward to returning to Catalina Cove, just to show them I'm not the chubby girl I used to be. It's been fifteen years."

Donna chuckled. "It might be fifteen years for you, but I returned several times with..." The name died on her lips.

"Go ahead and say it, Donna. You returned several times with Isaac. Saying his name won't kill you."

"It might," Donna said, getting out the car. For an unsettling moment, she felt a tightening of regret in her stomach. "Okay, I returned several times with Isaac to check on his father when he was alive."

Not long after she'd graduated from college, her parents had retired and pursued their dream of moving to Switzerland. As far as Donna was concerned, there was nothing in Catalina Cove, Louisiana for her anymore.

"Isaac is living in Boston, Donna. He might not even come."

"And there's a chance he might," Donna countered.

"Whatever. Just call me when you get home after checking through your mail."

"It doesn't matter," Donna said, walking briskly toward the salon. "I have no intention of returning to Catalina Cove for the holiday homecoming."

Hours later, after leaving the salon and stopping to do a few errands, Donna entered her home, closed the door behind her, and glanced around. A sense of loneliness surrounded her. Quickly shaking off the feeling, she placed her purse and the mail she'd grabbed from her mailbox on the table before removing her coat and hanging it in the closet.

It had been typical Seattle weather, with rain most of the day. Forecasters warned to expect colder days and snow by the weekend. Returning to where she'd placed the mail, she began going through it. Christmas cards, Christmas cards, and more Christmas cards, which she tossed aside to join others she'd recently received. Seeing all the cards just made her feel lonelier. The last few years, she sometimes hadn't even taken the time to open them. She would band them together and stick them in a box somewhere, out of sight and out of mind. It had been that way for her since her divorce.

She wished she could get in the Christmas spirit, but it was hard when she had no one to share the holidays with. She'd thought of flying to Switzerland to see her parents but knew not to bother. They would spend the entire time telling her what a mistake she'd made in divorcing Isaac.

She paused when she came to the card from the Catalina Cove High School Homecoming Committee; the one Nina was all excited about receiving. Sighing deeply, she opened the holiday invitation and only gave it a cursory glance before placing it back in the envelope. Like she'd told Nina, she had no plans to attend.

She was about to head toward her kitchen when her phone rang. She recognized Nina's ringtone. Answering the phone, Donna said, "Yes, I'm home. Yes, I checked my mail. And yes, I did get the invitation to the holiday homecoming. However, my answer is still no. Goodbye, Nina."

"Hey wait!"

Donna let out another deep sigh. "What?"

"Skype me on the tube."

Leaving the kitchen, Donna picked up her remote and turned on her Smart TV. She wasn't surprised to see her best friend standing in the middle of a very decorated living room. There was a huge Christmas tree, stockings hung from the fireplace, several life-size reindeer were standing by the tree, and Nina was wearing a Ms. Claus outfit.

Donna couldn't help but laugh. "Don't you think you overdid things?"

"Umm," Nina said straining her neck to see around Donna's home on Skype. "You're a fine one to talk. You haven't done anything at all."

"And I don't intend to." Donna glanced at her watch. "I need to grab something to eat before heading out to a Homeowners Association meeting."

"Do me a favor, Donna, and think about going home."

Home? She hadn't thought of Catalina Cove as a home for years and knew her friend felt the same way. Nina hadn't returned since her grandmother had died during her first year in college at UCLA. Both she and Nina had been eager to leave town after graduation, but for different reasons. Donna wanted to spend more time with Isaac at the university, away from the watchful eyes of their parents. Nina went off to school looking for a fresh start, in a place where she could leave all those "fat girl" jokes behind her. So why was she so anxious to go back now?

Donna glanced over at a framed picture of her and Isaac that had been taken years ago. The picture represented when the two were a happy couple. It had been during happier times. They were smiling for the camera and looked very much in love. And at the time, they had been. She'd kept the photo as a reminder of the biggest mistake she'd ever made—letting Isaac go.

"Donna, you know what I think?"

She glanced back at Nina on the television screen. Her friend probably knew where her gaze had drifted. "No, what do you think?"

"You haven't gotten over Isaac."

No news there, Donna thought. Of course, she hadn't gotten over Isaac. How could a woman get over a man who had once been her whole life? There was no need to lie about it. "No, I haven't gotten over him," she admitted.

"Then why are you doing this to yourself? It's been almost three years. You've deliberately not communicated with him in all this time. Why are you being so stubborn about it?"

"I am not being stubborn."

"Yes, you are. I've been your best friend since eighth grade, and I know what you're doing."

Donna didn't say anything for a minute, and then said, "You might see it as being stubborn, but I see it as a way to protect my heart. Our divorce was all my fault. I accept that now."

She paused. "I also accept that I deserve all the heartbreak I've endured. If I was to ever see Isaac with someone else, I doubt I'd be able to handle it, Nina. For all I know, he could be married again. Or even have children. He always wanted a family. That's just one of the promises I broke. I doubt he will ever forgive me. He told me he wouldn't."

"People say a lot of things in anger, Donna. You know that."

"Yes, but—"

"But nothing. I think it's time for you to do something before it's too late. What if Isaac isn't married or seriously involved with anyone?"

Donna rolled her eyes. "Do you honestly believe someone who looks like Isaac will still be single?"

"Yes, I do believe it, because someone who looks like you aren't involved with anyone, either."

Dating was something she didn't like to discuss with Nina. Her best friend went out a lot, in pursuit of the perfect guy. But Donna, who felt she'd had the perfect guy with Isaac, had adopted the attitude of 'why settle for less when you've had the best'. Dating, just for the fun of something to do, didn't make much sense to her.

"Can we change the subject, please, Nina?"

"Fine, but just think about it, okay? You can't just leave things this way between you and Isaac. You need to go back to Catalina Cove, in case Isaac decides to come to homecoming. And if he doesn't come, you need to contact him and tell him how you feel. It's never too late to say you're sorry."

Donna knew that just saying she was sorry would not be enough. Not even close. "Nina...."

"Fine, let's change the subject," Nina said. "So, how are things going at work?"

Donna shook her head, thinking about her job. She hadn't mentioned anything to Nina about being overlooked for a promotion she felt she was hers. She had worked for the company longer, handled way more accounts, and was definitely more qualified than the man who'd been promoted above her. "Things are going okay, I guess."

"You guess? Is there something you aren't telling me, Donna?"

Instead of answering with a lie, Donna said, "I need to get ready for my meeting. We'll talk later. Bye, Nina."

A short while later, after heating a dinner in the microwave and taking a shower, Donna dressed in a pair of jeans and a pullover sweater. Isaac had often said he liked seeing her in jeans. She liked seeing him in jeans, as well, she thought with a smile. But why was she thinking about him? He'd been on her mind a lot lately, remembering his likes and dislikes, his smiles and even his frowns...which she could easily remove when she'd set her mind to it. However, more than anything, she was remembering his expertise in the bedroom. If she never made love again with another man, she had more than enough memories of Isaac to satisfy her.

As Donna grabbed her purse off the table and headed out to the meeting, she couldn't help but recall what had happened to bring an end to a love that should have lasted forever.

Four years earlier

"You want to quit your job, Isaac?" Donna asked, quickly sitting up in bed, not believing what she was hearing. It was snowing outside, and this was one of the few nights she wasn't traveling—mainly because the storm had shut down the airport.

Isaac turned toward her, and she saw the lines of strain on his face. Where had they come from? Had they been there for a while, but she'd been too busy to notice? Like she'd been too busy for a lot of things regarding him lately?

Her job had become more and more demanding and she was killing herself trying to keep up. Mr. Chase had told her she could have an assistant, but he'd yet to authorize the position. If nothing else, she'd seen since becoming Advertising Manager, the more she did, the more she was expected to do. Sometimes she wondered if they assumed, she was a machine instead of a human being. She was handling far more accounts than her counterparts.

Donna got out of the bed and moved toward him. "Isaac, what's wrong? Why are you thinking of leaving your job?" She didn't want to mention the six-figure salary he earned. She didn't make that much now but figured another promotion or two would get her there.

He blew out a frustrated breath. "I've been telling you what's wrong for the past two months, Donna."

Had he? From the agitated look on his face, he'd obviously had, but she hadn't been listening. Evidently, she'd been paying more attention to her work than to her husband. "Then please tell me again, Isaac. What's going on?"

For a minute, she thought he wouldn't tell her anything. Then he admitted, "Ever since that guy from Atlanta took over the department, he's been making everybody's life a living hell. Especially mine. I've been written up twice in six months."

"Written up? You?" Isaac was a model employee. Stellar in every way. He had numerous "Employee of the Year" plaques on the wall to prove it.

"Yes, me. I'm ready to work for myself, Donna."

They'd had this discussion before. Over the years, they'd built a nice savings, but the capital needed to start his own business would consume most of it. "Isaac, I know you're upset, but starting your own company would take most of our savings."

"I got a call from Uncle Mark today."

Mark Elloran was Isaac's father's only brother, and he lived in Boston. Although the Elloran brothers had never gotten along, Mark had a good relationship with his only nephew. The man had been married years ago, but his wife had passed away before they'd had any children.

"And?" she asked.

"And he's offered me a partnership in his company."

Company? From what she recalled, Mark's 'company was nothing more than a computer repair service. It couldn't be doing that well. "Please don't tell me you're thinking about leaving your job and going to work for your uncle in Boston, Isaac."

"I won't be working for him, Donna. I will be a partner, and yes, I am considering it. It's something I want us to think about."

She suddenly felt a migraine coming on, something she'd been suffering from a lot lately; especially when she was under stress. "How can you even consider such a thing? I love my job. I can't just leave."

"Well, I don't love my job, and I think we should move somewhere that might benefit the both of us."

"And how will moving benefit *us* exactly? You'd be giving up a six-figure salary and I will be giving up one close to it."

"But we'll be working on something that could one day grow and become more successful than what we—"

"You don't know that, and I refuse to consider it," she interrupted to say. "It's not fair for you to even ask me to."

He looked at her for a long moment, then said, "Had you come to me and told me how much you dislike your job, that you felt you were not being treated fairly, but you had an opportunity to do something that might one day benefit us, and it would give you a chance to work for yourself...I'd go along with it, Donna. I would have had enough faith in you to believe you'd done your homework and knew that it would be a great move for us. Can you at least give me credit for doing that?"

When she didn't say anything, he pressed on. "If I thought it would make you happy, I would move to Timbuktu. I guess that means your happiness to me means more than my happiness to you."

Fury almost choked her. "That's not true and it's unfair for you to say that, Isaac."

From the look on his face, it was obvious his anger matched hers. In fact, he was angrier than she'd ever seen him before. "You want to know what's unfair, Donna?" he asked, taking a step toward her. His voice sent cold chills down her spine. "What's unfair is the shitty way you've been treating me lately. I've tried to be understanding when you work late or have to go out of town, sometimes at the last minute."

His words stung. "You said you understood, Isaac. That I had your support. You said you had my back."

He rubbed his hand down his face, as if it would ease some of his anger. Then, in a softer tone, he said, "I have given you my support, Donna. I've always had your back and I've even tried to understand why you prefer to hang out with your newfound "girlfriends" than spend time with me. But what I won't tolerate any longer is the way those women are filling your head with foolishness about how you should be handling me."

"They haven't been doing that," she protested.

"Haven't they?"

Yes, Carmen and Audrey had, but did Isaac think she was that easily influenced? She had ignored them when they said that men like her husband, liked to keep women under their thumb.

"I have a mind of my own, Isaac. And at the present time, my mind is telling me that quitting my job to follow you to Boston is not a good idea unless you can guarantee it won't hurt us financially. I like the money I'm making, and I like the money you're making. I also like the size of our savings. We've worked hard to get where we are."

"And I think moving to Boston will help us do better," he said.

She crossed her arms. "How? You're willing to give up a six-figure salary to work in a shop that fix computers?"

"My uncle's business is more than that. In fact, he's developing this—"

"Please spare me, Isaac," she cut in to say. "I've heard your father talk about his brother, and how he's always chasing the next bright idea. Are you willing to risk everything we've built for that?"

Instead of answering her, Isaac grabbed his jacket off the chair and left. This was a first for them. They'd never argued to the point where one of them walked out angry. Things weren't always great with her at work, but she knew how to tough it out. Obviously, Isaac didn't. She just couldn't understand how he'd think moving to Boston was the answer to his problems at work. How could he ask that of her? Ask that of them?

She felt tears sting her eyes. Maybe it was a good thing he had left. Hopefully, he would take a drive around town and come to his senses about uprooting them to Boston. At least, she hoped that's what he would do.

Chapter Four

Back to the present

I saac walked into Witherspoon Café and went to the first empty booth he saw. He didn't come here often, but when he did, he knew he would get delicious food and good service.

"Good morning, Isaac. You're in here early."

He smiled up at Bryce Witherspoon. "Good morning, Bryce. I promised Reid Lacroix that I'd install additional security cameras around his estate, and figured I'd get an early start."

She returned his smile. "I thought you moved back to the cove to enjoy retirement. That sounds like work to me. But then, I can't complain. The security equipment you installed on Eagle Bend Inlet saved my life."

He shook his head. "Kaegan's alertness and quick thinking is what saved your life."

"Yes, but you helped, too." As if that settled it, she asked, "You're having your usual?"

"Yes. Thanks."

She wrote down his order, then smiled again. "I'll be right back with your coffee."

When Bryce walked off, he glanced around the café. Bryce's parents owned the place and she helped them out on occasion. He liked Bryce. She was a beautiful woman. Then again, a number of beautiful women had graduated from Catalina Cove High School. He'd finished school with her oldest brother, Ry, and still considered him one of his best friends.

Bryce was engaged to marry Kaegan Chambray. Because Kaegan had been a loner around school, Isaac hadn't gotten to know him that well, but things changed when Isaac returned to the cove last year. Kaegan had been one of the first to welcome him back to town.

Isaac chuckled when he recalled Kaegan had also strongly hinted that Bryce was off limits...even though Kaegan and Bryce hadn't dated seriously in almost ten years. At the time Isaac figured Kaegan was operating on the premise that what was once his would always be his.

He'd wondered how Bryce would have felt had she known what Kaegan's stance had been. It didn't matter now because the two of them had worked things out and were back together. Kaegan was part of the Pointe-au-Chien Native American Tribe. His ancestors' ties to the cove and surrounding bayou went back generations.

That was one of the things Isaac liked about Catalina Cove. It contained a diverse group of people, even though there were a fair number of Creoles.

The cove's history was a required subject in school, so Isaac had known that both white refugees and free people of color had found sanctuary in the bayous. Some had lived among the Native Americans. A blend of French, Spanish, and African heritages, they'd come together to create their own culture—the Louisiana Creole.

He, himself, was a Louisiana Creole, a proud mixture of all three— French, Spanish and African. So was Donna. He'd been captivated by her beautiful brown eyes, high cheekbones, shoulder-length dark hair, and rich brown skin, the first time he'd noticed her in high school.

Her family had been part of the cove's upper middle class. Her father had been an Air Force pilot who later worked for a major airline. Though Isaac's parents never reached the status of upper middle class, he felt they lived a good life and didn't recall ever wanting for anything. His dad's profession as the town's repairman had kept him busy, and there'd been no shortage of food on the table.

Bryce placed his coffee in front of him, intruding into his thoughts. "Thanks."

"You're welcome, Isaac."

One of the cool things about the cove was that the majority of the kids that lived there got along, regardless of their social classes. Even if their parents were snobs, the young people had formed a united cohesive group. It was one of the reasons he was looking forward to the holiday homecoming. He hadn't seen some of his classmates in years; many not since graduation. And he hoped a number of them would come back for homecoming.

His thoughts shifted to Donna. She should have gotten her invitation by now. Would she come? How would he react if she did come? Although she'd practically cut all ties with him, he hadn't with her. Because he'd known how important the holidays were to her, he would send her a Christmas card every year. Although he was fairly certain she'd gotten them, she never acknowledged them. This year, he'd decided not to bother. She obviously didn't want to have anything to do with him.

She certainly got what she wanted, and anytime he thought about it, anger and pain consumed him. How could two people who'd once loved each other the way they had, allow miscommunication, unrealistic expectations and misplaced resentment to end things between them? Had she trusted him more and had more confidence in his dream for them, she could be here with him now, enjoying the benefits of everything he'd acquired in the past three years. Instead she'd given up on him, given up on them.

Donna hadn't wanted to move to Boston and they'd constantly argued about it. Eventually, they'd come up with a compromise—he would move to Boston without her and they would share weekends to visit each other. A long-distance marriage wasn't what he'd wanted, but it was the only thing she would agree to.

Things started off rocky and didn't get any better from there. Donna would catch a red-eye on Thursday night and arrive in Boston the Friday morning. Then she'd have to leave late on Sunday to be back in Seattle for Monday morning. They tried packing a lot into the hours they were together. He'd wanted to take her around Boston, to show her what a great city it was, and to hear how her week had gone. While apart, they talked every night but since she put in a lot of overtime, she'd sometimes fall asleep in the middle of their conversations.

He knew she was driving herself to exhaustion and he started to resent not being there to see her, hold her, and take care of her. Whenever he returned home, he had to put his foot down, making sure they spent time together and he wasn't competing with work she'd brought home. Whenever she came to Boston, he'd made it all about her and their time together, and he couldn't help getting annoyed that he wasn't receiving the same treatment when he traveled to Seattle.

Within six months of the arrangement, she began allowing her work to interfere with her visits to see him; cancelling her weeks to fly to Boston at the last minute and bringing work with her when she did come. Refusing to give up and ready to fight for their marriage, he would travel to Seattle on those occasions when she didn't come to him. However, when he got there, he'd often discovered she'd brought work home, which only made him angry. It also made him realize she was no longer as invested in their marriage as he was.

"Mind if I join you, Isaac?"

He glanced up to see Kaegan. In a way, he was glad his friend had appeared when he had. Isaac was getting upset again, thinking of how Donna had chosen her career over him. "Sure, have a seat. Where's Ray and Sawyer this morning?" he asked. Kaegan, Ray Sullivan and Sawyer Grisham were close friends and usually met every morning at the café for breakfast.

"Sawyer relieved one of his deputies last night and worked the night shift, and Ray is helping Ashley with the twins today. They have a doctor's visit."

Sawyer was the sheriff of Catalina Cove and Ray's wife had given birth to twins over a month ago. Isaac could see how they had their hands full. "Have you seen the babies, yet?"

Kaegan grinned. "Yes. And although they have Ashley's eyes, the rest of their features I firmly blame on Ray."

Isaac nodded, thinking of his and Donna's plan to have children. If things had worked out the way they were supposed to, they might have had at least one child by now. "How are the responses coming back for homecoming?" he asked.

"Pretty good. But if you're asking because you're wondering about Donna, the answer is no, Isaac. We haven't heard anything from her."

A keen sense of disappointment tugged at his insides. In a way, he was hoping she would come. Why he felt that way, he wasn't sure. All he knew was that he *needed* to see her again.

Three years ago, when she'd cancelled yet another visit out to see him, he'd had enough. He'd told her he was tired of competing against her job and making all the concessions in their marriage, and that when she decided she truly wanted their marriage to work, she would know where to find him. A month later, he'd received divorce papers, citing "irreconcilable differences".

Then why did he want to see her again so badly—the woman who'd broken his heart, the woman who hadn't wanted to be his wife? He knew the answer, but his pride wouldn't let him say it, even to himself. Besides, for all he knew, she could be involved in a serious relationship. How would he handle it if she brought some guy with her? He knew she hadn't remarried since one of the conditions of the divorce had been that she could continue to live in their home as long as she remained unmarried. Donna getting married would be a game-changer.

"When do you start work at Reid's place?" Kaegan asked him.

"Today. That's why I'm up so early."

"Good morning Kaegan," Bryce greeted, coming to their table. "Your usual?" She was all smiles and the look she had for her fiancé was something to see. He recalled Donna once looking at him that way.

Isaac glanced at Kaegan and saw a similar smile spread across his lips. "Yes, baby, the usual."

Bryce nodded and walked off. Kaegan watched her go and continued to stare even after she'd gone into the kitchen and was no longer in sight. It was as if he was planning to sit there and wait until she reappeared. Isaac had to clear his throat to get his attention.

Kaegan looked over at him, chuckled and said, "Sorry about that."

"No need to apologize." He knew that Kaegan and Bryce were planning a summer wedding. "Do you think you're going to last until June?"

"There's no way. That's why I am working on her to change it."

"Your wedding day?" Isaac asked, looking at Kaegan over the rim of his coffee cup.

A roguish smile curved Kaegan's lips. "Yes. If I had my way, we'd get married before Christmas."

He believed Kaegan. Isaac remembered how anxious he'd been to marry Donna. It had helped that they'd lived together the last two years of college, but he hadn't been content until he'd put a permanent wedding band on her finger.

"Isaac?"

He glanced up to find Kaegan staring at him. "Yes?"

"I know how it is when a man still loves a woman, even when he doesn't want to admit it. I went through it for ten years before finally getting back with Bryce. I wouldn't wish that wasted time on anyone. I hope if Donna comes to town for the school's homecoming, that the two of you can fix things."

"You think I still love her?"

"Don't you? You're one of the most eligible bachelors in town, yet you live the life of a loner. I did the same thing, because even though I didn't want to admit it, I knew in my gut that no woman could ever have my heart like Bryce."

Isaac didn't say anything for a moment, and then he said. "The difference with you and Bryce is that you were angry with her for what you *thought* she did. I *know* exactly what Donna did. She chose her career over me. That's a bitter pill to swallow."

"Yes, but you might have to swallow it, if you want a second chance with her."

Isaac took a sip of his coffee. "And what makes you think I want a second chance with Donna?"

Kaegan leaned back in his chair and studied him a little too long to suit Isaac, but he wanted to hear what Kaegan had to say. "Because I've been where you are now, and I see the signs, Isaac. You're chomping at the bit, not knowing if she's coming home or not. A part of you wants to see her but another part doesn't. At this moment, the part that wants to see her is winning."

Kaegan was right. That part was winning...but he intended to fight it with every ounce of pride that he had left. Donna had hurt him, and he wasn't going to give her the chance to do it again.

"Please tell me you've changed your mind about going, Donna."

Donna took a deep breath to the point she risked the buttons on her blouse popping from an expanding cleavage. Nina usually didn't call her at work—she was usually far too busy at the hospital. And those odd times when she did, it was usually to tell her about a recent date. Over the years, Nina had kissed her share of frogs who'd never turned out to be princes.

Getting up from the chair behind her desk, Donna walked over to the window. It was another rainy day in Seattle. "No, I haven't changed my mind, Nina. But just because I'm missing homecoming, there's no reason for you not to go."

"Honestly Donna, how can you even suggest something like that?"

Easily. That response would be a quick one off her tongue if she'd been asked that question by anyone else. But this wasn't anyone else. This was her best friend. Donna had always thought Nina was pretty, even when she had carried those extra pounds as a teen. While other kids had only seen her weight, Donna had loved the beautiful, bright, and intelligent person that Nina was.

Her best friend had gone to a college as far from the cove as she could get, only returning in her freshman year for her grandmother's funeral. Now Nina was older, more beautiful, she weighed a lot less and had a new attitude about life. She'd found all that self-esteem she'd lost during her high school years and was taking no prisoners.

In a way, Donna understood Nina's desire to go back to Catalina Cove—to face down those classmates who'd ridiculed her about her weight problem. For years, she'd tried to convince Nina to just let it go, to forget about the people who'd been cruel back then and hoped they'd changed over the years. But it hadn't mattered to Nina. It was as if Catalina Cove was the one thing in her past she needed to get beyond before she could fully move on.

But then, Donna also knew how much Nina had changed over the years. She was no longer the shy girl who'd let insults hurt her. She'd not only grown a backbone, but her self-image, confidence and faith in herself had grown in proportion. It had taken years—and even therapy—but she had it now. The only challenge left for Nina to overcome was to go back to where it had all started for her—Catalina Cove.

Donna walked back to her desk to sit down. Catalina Cove was where it had all started for her, as well. Falling in love with Isaac, their walks on the beach, their boat rides around the Moulden River and the picnics along the lake. There was so much about the cove she loved, and Isaac had been a major part of it.

"I would like to give you more time to think about it, Donna, but airline ticket prices are increasing every day; especially as we get closer to the holidays."

Donna knew that no matter what she said, Nina was determined not to give up on her, hope she would change her mind, regardless of how many times Donna said 'no'.

"Doesn't how I feel matter?" she asked, with annoyance in her voice.

"How you feel *would* matter, if I thought returning to Catalina Cove was a bad thing for you. But I don't see it that way. You were the most popular girl in our graduating class. Everyone liked you. People will expect you to be there."

"And most will expect me and Isaac to still be married."

There was a pause and Nina then asked, "Is that what this is all about Donna? You don't want to go back because you're embarrassed that you and Isaac are no longer together?"

"Nothing lasts forever, Nina."

"I know that, but do you? Truly? I know you're afraid of seeing Isaac, should he show up. But instead of being afraid, maybe you need to get up the courage to tell him how you feel."

Donna absently threw paperclips on her desk, thinking Nina had suggested that very thing before. "And how do you think I feel?"

"We've covered this before, but if you need to hear it again, here goes. I think you feel like a woman who deep down inside wants to own up to her one big mistake in life. Isaac loved you."

"You act like I didn't love him," Donna snapped.

"Maybe not more than your career."

Donna went still. Nina had just repeated the same accusation Isaac had leveled at her several times during the final months of their marriage. She had loved Isaac more than life. But she had to admit, she *had* gotten caught up in her career. And in the end, she'd lost him.

"Isaac had become a distraction, but I never loved my career more than him, Nina. You should know that."

"Your actions told another story during that time, Donna. And please explain to me how a man you supposedly loved could become a distraction."

Donna nibbled on her bottom lip. If Nina couldn't understand what she'd been going through back then, how could she ever expect Isaac to understand how for so long, she'd built her life around him; but when she'd got a challenging job, one she'd loved, all she could think about was moving up the corporate ladder. She'd become more than driven. She'd become obsessed with being successful at something other than being his wife.

Instead of giving Nina an answer, she said. "I need to start thinking about what I want."

"You remember what Diana Ross said in *Mahogany* don't you?" Nina asked her.

Donna rolled her eyes. How could she not know? That had been Nina's grandmother's favorite movie and she would watch the video over and over again. When she and Nina had been kids, they would often sit and watch it with her. Eventually, it had become one of their favorite movies as well.

"Yes. Success is nothing, unless you have the person you love to share it with," Donna said, stating Billy D. Williams' iconic line from the movie.

"I rest my case, Donna, since we both know what you want...or more specifically, *who* you want."

"What if he brings someone with him to homecoming? I'm not sure I'll be able to handle it."

"You'll just have to accept that if he does bring someone, he has every right to do so, just like you'd have every right to bring someone, as well. So, are you going to homecoming or not?"

Donna could think of so many ways things could go wrong. But there was also a chance that things could go right. She couldn't operate on the illusion that all they had to do was kiss and make-up. There had been too much hurt, pain, and anger for that. But if he were to come to homecoming, at least she would find inner peace knowing he was happy, even if he was happy without her. The question of the hour, and the one Nina was forcing her to ask herself, was...could she find the strength to find that out and face whatever the answer might be?

She sighed and then said. "Yes, Nina. I'll go to the holiday home-coming."

Chapter Five

Welcome to Catalina Cove Senior High School's Holiday Homecoming

Donna glanced at the huge lighted sign as she entered the Roberta Lacroix Civic Center. The building was a new addition to town, built a few years ago by Reid LaCroix, the wealthiest man in the cove, in memory of his late wife. In the massive lobby was a gigantic beautifully decorated Christmas tree. The sound of holiday music flowed through several speakers.

Instead of heading straight for the ballroom where the event would take place, she pulled her cell phone out of her purse as she made a quick right to a hallway where smaller banquet rooms were located. She glanced at her watch, then punched in Nina's phone number.

Donna and Nina had planned to arrive in New Orleans around the same time and share the one-hour car ride to the cove. However, when Donna had landed in New Orleans, she'd received a text from Nina saying her flight had been delayed, and that she wouldn't be arriving until later.

"Hello?"

"Nina? Have you made it to town?" Donna asked. People were arriving but she wasn't ready to go inside the ballroom yet. She and Nina had planned to go in together.

"I'm walking into Grammie's house now. I was just about to text you. I'll be there as soon as I shower and change."

"Are you okay?" Donna asked. This was the first time Nina had been in her Grammie's house since the funeral years ago, even though she'd decided not to sell it. Bryce Witherspoon, a local realtor in town, had been hired as property manager to keep it rented out with responsible tenants.

Because so many people had arrived in town for homecoming, the hotels in the cove were packed. It hadn't helped matters that Donna and Nina had decided to come at the last minute. Luckily, Bryce had informed Nina that her grandmother's house was currently vacant and suggested they stay there.

Donna hadn't wanted to leave the house before Nina arrived, but since Nina had had no idea when that would be, she had encouraged Donna to go ahead without her. She'd promised to join Donna at the civic center later.

"Yes, I'm okay, although it felt strange walking through the door knowing Grammie wasn't here. But I'm fine now. Being here makes me realize how much I miss Catalina Cove."

Donna had felt the same way. Although she'd been back to the cove more frequently than Nina while married to Isaac, it had been at least seven years since her last visit. She'd been overcome by a sense of nostalgia the moment she'd driven into town. There was nothing like Christmas in Catalina Cove. All the merchants had bright colorful lights covering their storefronts, and the city's street lanterns had been decorated with wreaths and holly. Catalina Cove had always been considered a shipping town and seeing all the vessels that lined the shipping district, she guessed that hadn't changed much. She was glad to see the town had retained its small-town charm.

Everyone born in the cove knew the town's history. This parcel of land that sat on the gulf had been a gift to the notorious pirate, Jean Lafitte, for his role in helping the United States fight the British during the War of 1812. There were some who believed Lafitte had been buried at sea in the waters surrounding Catalina Cove. Those same people believed there was a lot of buried treasure around the cove as well. So many outsiders had arrived with treasure maps, determined to find all the buried loot, that the elected officials of Catalina Cove had to step in. They believed that if there was buried treasure somewhere around the cove, then it was to stay buried. If found, any treasure would become the property of Catalina Cove.

"Being here makes me realize how much I miss this place, as well," Donna said, sighing. "So much looks the same. The moment I drove into town, I felt like I was home. We were born here, Nina. And we spent so much of our lives here. Christmas in the cove was the best."

"Hey, don't forget the Shrimp Festival and the Blueberry Festival," Nina reminded her.

Nina was right. She couldn't forget those. Catalina Cove was the best place for seafood, especially big, plump delicious shrimp. And it was also considered the blueberry capital in the country. The best tasting blueberries were grown, harvested and shipped right from here.

"Let me go so I can shower and change. I'll see you in a little bit."

"Do you want me to wait outside for you?" Donna asked.

"No need to do that, Donna. I'll find you when I get there."

"Okay." Donna clicked off the phone. This was probably for the best. Nina needed to make a grand entrance. Her best friend deserved to stun the crowd with her transformation. Everyone would immediately see the physical one, but by the end of the evening, they would see the mental one as well.

Homecoming was a weekend affair with the dance kicking things off tonight. Tomorrow was the picnic, a Christmas tree lighting and an ice cream social. Then on Sunday, there was a special church service with dinner afterwards at the Witherspoon Café.

Donna had made plans to fly back to Seattle on Monday to return to work on Tuesday. Nina was staying for a week to visit some of her grandmother's neighbors and go through her grandmother's belongings that she'd put in storage years earlier.

Donna could hear a band playing the school song, which meant the dance was about to start. Not ready to be seen yet, she decided to go to the ladies' room first and check her appearance. She turned quickly to go down another corridor...and hit what felt like a huge solid wall. Immediately, she realized it wasn't a wall but a man. The moment his hand reached out and touched her arm to keep her from falling, a rush of heated desire clawed at her insides. Even before tilting her head back to stare up at him, she knew who had touched her. The man who used to have the right to touch her all over. A flash of heat rushed through her at the memory of all the ways that he'd done just that.

The hall was empty, and she appreciated there weren't others around. She wasn't certain what his reaction would be upon seeing her. Would he be angry? The last time she'd seen him, he had been. Regardless, she'd known there was a chance they might run into each other and intended to make this as pleasant as possible.

Drawing in a deep breath, she forced a smile to her lips. "Hello Isaac."

Isaac's heart skipped a few beats as he stared down into the face of the woman, he'd thought he could never live without. And yet, somehow, he'd done just that for the past three years. She was as beautiful now as she'd been the first time he saw her—when he'd walked into his science class at Catalina Cove High School and noticed her in a way he hadn't before.

He always liked the way she wore her hair, with the silky mass of black hair flowing to her shoulders. And her chocolate brown eyes, high cheekbones and the luscious texture of her café-au-lait skin still took his breath away.

People often said she could be a double for Zoë Kravitz, but he'd always been quick to argue that it was the other way around. Zoë Kravitz could be a double for his wife. Now his ex-wife.

He'd wondered how he would react upon seeing her. Would he be filled with anger or would he feel nothing at all? When he'd arrived, he was hoping he would feel nothing at all, but right now all he felt was overwhelmed by his complete awareness of her. It was somehow shocking his nervous system, making him realize that some things never changed. And his reaction to Donna topped the list.

"Hello, Donna. I heard you were coming, but I honestly didn't think that you would," he said, not able to take his eyes off the face that could still hold him captivated.

"And why wouldn't I come, Isaac?"

He shrugged, dismissing the sting in her voice while thinking that he could come up with a number of reasons. However, instead of stating them, he said, "No reason."

He forced the reasons they had gotten a divorce to the back of his mind. When he'd learned she would be coming, he'd spent countless sleepless nights trying to be fair and see things from her perspective. But he still couldn't. The bottom line was that she had chosen her career over him. She had given up on him when he'd done everything he could to accommodate her.

All that was water under the bridge now. Before leaving home tonight, he had promised himself that he wouldn't let the past weigh him down. He would be civil to her, no matter what she did or said. Still, he couldn't deny that he was glad to see her. Over the years, he had thought of her often, sometimes endlessly. And now that he was standing here, looking in her gorgeous face, he could admit that although he'd tried to move on with his life, he hadn't.

"How have you been Donna?"

She seemed surprised that he'd asked and had to be wondering why he was still holding on to her arm. Did his touch affect her the way just touching her was affecting him after all this time? And why did she have to look so damn beautiful in that short green dress that was showing what a gorgeous pair of legs she had?

"I've been fine, Isaac. What about you?"

"I'm doing okay. I'm surprised you could get away for this. I know how busy you are with your job..." he couldn't resist saying, finally releasing her arm.

He would have to ask about her job, Donna thought. The same job she'd chosen over him. But then, hadn't he chosen his uncle's business over her? She knew that wasn't true. Even after moving to Boston, he had gone out of his way to make things work between them. She needed to own up to the fact that she'd been the one who'd failed them, not him.

"My work is going well, Isaac." There was no need to tell him she'd only got one more promotion since their split and had been passed over for the one she felt she rightly deserved.

"That's good to hear."

She honestly doubted that, since her job had been a bone of contention between them. "Is it?"

"Yes. I only wanted what was best for you. Whatever made you happy."

Was that why he hadn't contested the divorce? For the longest time, a part of her felt that although she'd filed for the divorce, he'd given in too easily. But another part of her had known she'd pushed him beyond his limit. Everybody had a breaking point and she'd found his.

At that moment, though, she couldn't help but realize exactly what she'd lost. Standing before her was a man who looked good dressed in a dark gray business suit, white shirt and coordinating tie. Her gaze roamed over his features, taking in everything about him—the way his brows arched perfectly over a pair of piercing dark eyes; his strong jaw line; the most gorgeous pair of lips any man had a right to possess and skin the color of rich mocha.

Isaac Elloran had been every girl's dream. She had noticed him in school long before he'd noticed her. Her crush on him had been consuming, even though most of the other girls had a crush on him as well. He'd been the all-around guy everyone had liked. He would walk the halls with a smile that was like a magnet, drawing people to him. But he hadn't been flirty, nor had he been considered a player.

It had been three years since their divorce and Donna often wondered how they would react if they ever saw each other again. Tonight, she was finding out. Isaac still had the ability to send tingles through her body and make her appreciate being a woman, although he was no longer her man. Still, she couldn't dismiss his slow and sexy charm or the way he could look at a girl with those bedroom eyes, making her wish he would take her there...to a bedroom.

When things had gotten quiet between them—and she noticed him checking her out in much the same way she'd been doing to him—she decided to ask about his employment since he'd asked about hers. She would admit for a full year after his move, she had expected him to return to Seattle because he'd missed his six-figure salary. Evidently, she'd been wrong about that.

Breaking the silence between them, she asked, "What about your uncle's computer company? How's that going?"

He met her gaze. "A major electronic corporation came in and made me and Uncle Mark an offer we couldn't refuse. So, we sold the company."

Donna figured she had to look thunderstruck. "Your uncle's company was sold?"

"Yes. Thanks to a gadget he'd spent nearly a lifetime working on. It turned out to be a breakthrough component in the field of space aeronautics and worth millions. After selling the business, we left Boston. Uncle Mark bought a nice place in the Bahamas and I moved back here."

"To Catalina Cove?"

"Yes, a year ago. I've always wanted to come back here one day, you know that."

"Yes, but that was after retirement."

"I am retired."

She was shocked again. "You're retired?"

He smiled and a dimple appeared in his cheek. "Officially, yes. However, I find stuff to do to stay busy."

Isaac knew Donna would be surprised to learn he'd retired at thirty-four. It was funny how things had turned out. The computer company she had opposed him co-owning had ended up making millions, pretty much setting him and his uncle up real nice for the rest of their lives.

"Congratulations, Isaac. I'm glad things are working out so well for you. Now if you will excuse me, I need to go to the ladies' room."

He stepped back. "It was good seeing you again, Donna."

Isaac watched her walk away, still blown away by how good she looked in that dress. Drawing in a deep breath, he let it out slowly as he wondered if she was involved with anyone. He hadn't asked and she hadn't said. She didn't seem to be with anyone tonight. Did that mean anything?

His shoulders slumped somewhat at the thought that there could be a man in her life, serious or otherwise. It wasn't his business, but he'd admit the thought of her with someone else bothered him. "Get a grip, Elloran. Donna is no longer your problem," he muttered to himself.

Turning toward the ballroom, he discovered he couldn't move. It was as if his feet were solidly rooted in place. Obviously, he wasn't ready to let her go yet. Once they parted, given the status of their relationship, she might feel uncomfortable with them being seen together tonight. People might even begin to wonder if perhaps a reconciliation was in the works. He didn't want anyone to think that, any more than she did. Then again, he didn't give a damn what anyone thought.

It would be hard to go into that ballroom and pretend she was just another classmate that he hadn't seen in a while, to pretend they hadn't once meant everything to each other. That he didn't know her body, the one he found still so desirable, in ways no other man here tonight could claim.

He knew at that moment that he needed to see her again before going into the ballroom and getting lost in the crowd. With his mind made up, he leaned back against the wall and waited for her.

The moment Donna entered the ladies' room, she checked under the stalls and was glad to find them empty. Bracing against the vanity, she sighed deeply, trying to get all those tingling sensations to leave her body. She honestly shouldn't be surprised at the effect seeing Isaac again had on her.

There was so much she had wanted to say but couldn't. It was too late now. But that hadn't stopped her from remembering how things used to be between them. How powerful his shoulders felt beneath her fingertips, how mouthwatering he looked in a pair of briefs or when he wasn't wearing anything at all. Then there was the feel of his skin rubbing against hers or how they would take baths together and end up sloshing water all over the floor when they'd make love instead.

Forcing those thoughts from her mind, she tried thinking about what he'd told her about the company he'd owned with his uncle. She was happy for him. Retired at thirty-four. Wow! He said the company he and his uncle sold had made millions—the same company she'd tried talking him out of joining. The same company that had been a big reason for their divorce. No, it hadn't been the company, but her refusal to believe in him. She couldn't believe that leaving Seattle and moving to Boston was smart. Maybe that was why she hadn't kept her side of the compromise the way she should have.

There was no use crying over spilled milk now. But then, why not? Now was just as good a time as any. If it hadn't been for Nina, who was probably on her way, Donna would leave the reunion, then stop by the cove's wine store, go back to Nina's grandmother's house and have a pity party.

Not only was Isaac doing well and looking good, he'd smelled good, too. He still wore what she considered his signature fragrance—the cologne she'd introduced him to years ago by buying his first bottle. Months after he'd left, their home was still filled with his scent. Then one day she'd awakened, and it was gone.

There was a time she had loved him more than anything. More than her favorite pair of gym sneakers, her obsession with those blueberry muffins at Witherspoon Café and her crush on Usher. She would see him walking down the school's halls and her heart would go into overdrive. And when he'd smiled at her, she'd thought she had died and gone to heaven. He been handsome, muscular, athletic, and really, really hot.

She would never forget that day in her science class when he'd deliberately stayed behind to ask if he could walk her home. Of course, she'd said yes, and things had started that day. Word had quickly spread around school that she was Isaac Elloran's girl, and they'd been practically inseparable from that moment on.

Getting up her nerve, she quickly used the facilities and then walked out of the ladies' room. She'd get through tonight, somehow. All she needed to do was slip into the ballroom and wait for Nina. They'd spend a few hours talking with old friends, and then she'd leave. Period. She tried to push thoughts of Isaac out of her mind but couldn't. She had loved him once, and in truth, she still did. It didn't matter. What mattered was trying to hold onto her sanity tonight. He hadn't seemed to have been with anyone, but as far as she knew, his girlfriend could have been waiting for him in the ballroom. She hadn't asked, not wanting to hear the answer. If he was with someone tonight, she would handle it and keep her cool. She truly didn't have any choice in the matter.

Rounding the corner, Donna's breath caught when she saw that Isaac was still there, leaning against the wall in one hell of a sexy pose.

And it was obvious he was waiting for her.

Chapter Six

The click of heels on the tile floor made Isaac glance up. Donna still had that walk, the one that would turn guys' heads and make the lower parts of their body ache. He'd walked beside her with pride and a knowledge those other guys didn't have—like what turned her on, just what her skin felt, how beautiful she looked totally naked, and how her eyes would darken to a stormy brown during the heat of passion, right before she released that little catchy moan in her throat. And oh God, how she tasted... He paused in thought, tempted to lick his lips as tingles of desire extended through him.

But their connection hadn't been just about sex. Just as important to him were the times she was simply being Donna—his sweet, thoughtful, desirable, and seductive Donna. He remembered how she would curl in his lap and hum some romantic song, or she'd surprise him with a weekend getaway when she'd known he'd had a bad week at work. Or when she would lick the underside of his ear, telling him without words that she wanted to make love. Those had been the days when she'd had plenty of time for him and he hadn't had to compete for her attention.

Isaac forced those thoughts away. They were in the past and for the moment, he wanted them to stay there. Right now, he had to hold it together, even as emotions he'd managed to keep in check for the past three years rushed through him, bombarding him with memories of what they had once meant to each other.

43

"Isaac, you didn't have to wait for me."

She was wrong—he'd had no other option. He hadn't been able to leave knowing that once when they parted, he might not get a chance to talk to her again, be close enough to hear her voice, inhale her scent. "I wanted to wait. I hope you don't mind."

She tilted her head. "Why?"

He shoved his hands into his pockets. He could tell her the truth. But how could he explain that just seeing her again was doing things to his mind, not to mention his body. That being here in Catalina Cove, the place where their love had been born, and at Christmas time, was doing things to him—things he hadn't counted on. But he couldn't tell her that. Not now. Maybe not ever. So, instead, he said, "Because we need to catch up. How's everyone in Seattle? And what about Nina? I'm surprised she's not here with you."

Donna couldn't figure out why Isaac wanted to stand in a corridor and make small talk. He obviously wasn't in any more of a hurry to go inside the ballroom than she was. Did that mean he didn't have anyone waiting for him?

"Everyone in Seattle is fine," she said. "Stan got a huge job offer as a television executive, and he and Carmen moved to Atlanta."

He nodded. "Good for them."

Yes, good for them. She tried not to remember that Carmen had been one of her many so-called friends who'd told Donna that she couldn't let her husband's job take her away from Seattle. Funny, how Carmen hadn't hesitated to follow Stan to Atlanta. Losing Isaac was the price Donna had to pay for listening to her friends instead of Isaac. When Donna had asked Carmen about the move, she admitted to not wanting to go, but she'd said her husband was going places and she wanted to be beside him when he did.

Donna realized that had been the problem. *Her* problem. She'd honestly thought becoming a partner in Mark Elloran's company would not take Isaac anywhere. It would be like starting over and counting pennies again.

She'd been wrong. He was apparently living a good life in Catalina Cove, while she was busting her butt trying to get to the next level, that elusive promotion that seemed farther and farther away these days, no matter how hard she worked.

Now she couldn't help but recall that out of all her so-call friends, Nina had been the only one who'd encouraged her to think of her marriage and consider moving to Boston with Isaac. She had never stopped being Team Isaac.

"Nina's flight was late, but she'll be arriving later."

"Good. I'm looking forward to seeing her again."

Donna knew he was being sincere. He'd always liked Nina, even back when they'd been in high school together. More than once, he'd stepped in when Nina was being harassed by other classmates—usually the school's three notorious bullies, Rita, Monique, and Faye.

Nina was the only one of her friends he'd really liked and all through the years, he'd supported their friendship. The others he'd merely tolerated. "Nina is looking forward to coming here tonight."

He nodded and chuckled. "Yes, and I can guess why."

She chuckled as well. "Oh, come on, Isaac. You can do better than guess."

Anyone looking at them would never dream they were a divorced couple, the way they were standing there having a friendly conversation. But that's how it had always been with them. They could never stay angry at each other for long.

"Ready to go inside?"

Did he expect her to walk into the ballroom with him by her side? She could just imagine what people would think. It would definitely cause speculation about the state of their relationship, and she couldn't deal with that right now. She was certain word had gotten around about their divorce. She didn't want anyone thinking they were getting back together.

She was about to tell Isaac she'd go into the ballroom on her own, when a voice behind her stopped her.

"Well, well, if it isn't Isaac and Donna—Catalina Cove's version of Barbie and Ken. Funny seeing the two of you together. I'd heard you'd gotten a divorce."

Donna turned to look at Alicia Crawford and wasn't surprised to see she was still drop-dead gorgeous. And still a bitch. Even after all these years, it was apparent Alicia hadn't gotten over the fact that Isaac, the most popular boy at school, captain of the majority of the sport teams, the one voted class president, hadn't shown any interest in her, the girl voted the prettiest. She'd felt she could have any boy she'd wanted... and oh how she'd wanted Isaac. To this day, Donna had always been grateful that Isaac had chosen her over her nemesis.

Forcing a smile, Donna said, "Hello Alicia. Good seeing you again." She crossed her fingers behind her back because she'd just told a whopper of a lie.

"I live in Los Angeles now," Alicia said, fluffing her long black hair back from her shoulders, as if trying to create a dramatic effect.

"That's nice," Donna said, hoping she sounded as if she honestly didn't give a hoot.

"I'm sure you've seen all my television commercials," Alicia added, bragging as usual. "I understand they're shown a lot here in the cove."

Donna forced a smile. "I wouldn't know. I don't live here anymore."

Alicia smiled knowingly. "That's right, you don't." She then turned her full attention to Isaac. "But I heard that you've moved back."

Isaac nodded. "Yes, I have."

Donna noticed the flutter of a pulse at the base of his throat. Only someone who'd once been as close to Isaac as she had been would recognize the telltale sign of annoyance. In a way, she was glad that Alicia's antics weren't working on Isaac any more now than they had back when they'd been in high school.

Alicia had known Donna was Isaac's girlfriend, yet she'd flirted with him every chance she got. She'd even tried causing trouble, saying she could take Isaac from her anytime she wanted. Things had gotten so bad that Isaac had had to intervene, letting Alicia know in front of her friends that Donna was the girl he wanted.

"It's great that you've moved back," Alicia said happily, all but clapping her hands. "I plan to hang around town to visit the folks for a week. Since you're now a *free* man, maybe we can get together before I leave to return to California. For old time's sake."

Not waiting for Isaac to agree, Alicia walked off, swishing her hips in an outfit that showed more skin than fabric. "Well, I guess you have something to look forward to," Donna said, trying to keep the jealousy she felt from coming through in her voice. "It seems Alicia intends to make you her target, just like the good old days," she added.

Isaac stared down at her for a minute, then he said, "I'm really glad you decided to come tonight, Donna. Maybe Alicia will think we're getting back together and leave me alone."

Donna rolled her eyes. "Do you honestly think that will stop her, Isaac? She's a woman on the prowl. It's obvious she hasn't changed much since high school and figures she's entitled to have anyone she wants. And Alicia's been itching to get in your pants for years. Now she sees her chance."

"Not if you're with me."

"Aren't you with someone tonight?"

"No. I came alone to spend time with old friends, not to get stalked by Alicia. Umm, I've got a plan."

She remembered how, for as long as she'd known him, making a plan had always been the first thing he did when faced with a problem. "And what is this plan?"

"If anyone asks, we'll say we're thinking about getting back together."

"What!" Donna couldn't believe he would suggest such a thing. Alicia wouldn't be the only one they'd be deceiving. "And when that never happens, what then?" she asked. He had to know that this was a bad idea as much as she did.

"We'll worry about that later."

"Later?"

"Yes. Let's just get through tonight, shall we?"

Get through tonight? She didn't think so. Alicia was his problem, not hers. But then, the woman in her didn't want it to be just his problem. When Alicia had seen them together and still came on to Isaac—with Donna standing right there—she'd totally disrespected her. Even if they were divorced, any decent person, someone with an ounce of scruples, would not have done what Alicia had. Donna had tolerated Alicia's foolishness in high school, but she wasn't about to take it now. Nina wasn't the only one who'd grown a backbone.

"You think your plan will work?" she asked.

He reached out and took her hand in his, causing her breath to wobble a little when his long fingers entwined with hers. A degree of desire she hadn't felt in a long time—three years, in fact—spread through her. "Yes. Just follow my lead."

She frowned up at him. "I remember you saying that same thing, the first time we cut school together in our senior year. Your dad came home from his shop unexpectedly and caught us."

He chuckled. "You remember that?"

She rolled her eyes. "How could I forget? My parents threatened to take me to the doctor to make sure I wasn't pregnant, although we'd told them we hadn't done anything."

"We hadn't done anything *yet*," he emphasized while grinning mischievously. "If I recall, later that night, we snuck out and finished what we'd almost got caught doing."

Yes, they had and the memory of their first sexual encounter still made her breasts tingle. She looked up at him. "Okay Isaac Elloran, I will follow your lead tonight, but you'd better not get me into any trouble."

He smiled down at her. "I promise that I won't."

Isaac had promised his ex-wife that he wouldn't get her in trouble, but he hadn't promised to behave. The one thing he suddenly remembered was how to push Donna's sexual buttons, and for some reason he wanted to push every last one of them tonight. They'd been apart for nearly three years and he wanted to see if he could still get her worked up...the way she was getting him excited, without even trying.

Donna was one of the most sensuous women he'd ever known and that hadn't changed with time. She had more passion in her pinky finger than most women had in their entire bodies. Nor had anything changed in the looks area. She was still beautiful and tonight, she looked gorgeous.

They had a good evening, seeing old high school friends. More than one classmate had come up to them and said they still looked good together. Most people had heard of their divorce, but many of them stated it was good to see they were still friends and were counting on them getting back together.

Isaac made a reconciliation between them even more believable by holding her hand, whispering in her ear, or draping an arm around her shoulders. He loved the pretense, maybe a little too much, but couldn't help it. He still desired his ex-wife. Everything about her turned him on. Her nearness, her scent, and the heat of her skin. Enjoying the contact, he kept the palm of his hand plastered against the center of her spine.

Regardless of what Alicia Crawford thought, the woman couldn't hold a candle to Donna. Alicia never could and never would. Not that the woman hadn't tried a few times tonight. Even with Donna by his side, Alicia was still making herself a nuisance.

He was glad when one of her old boyfriends, Todd Filmore, a guy who'd been divorced three times and was still looking for the perfect woman, had come to snag Alicia for a dance. Isaac was grateful she hadn't come back.

"That was interesting. I never dreamed Rita, Monique, and Faye would get up in front of everyone to apologize," Donna said.

Isaac nodded in agreement. "It was surprising."

The three women had been notorious bullies around school. Now fifteen years later, they had returned to Catalina Cove to seek forgiveness for their behavior all those years ago. Rita, now a mother of one, was a high school principal in Mississippi; Monique was a dentist and mother of three living in Texas; and Faye was a businesswoman and mother of two living in Oklahoma. All three women looked good and when they'd entered the ballroom together, the room had become very quiet. It was obvious some of their previous victims hadn't known whether to stand still or run for cover.

But the three bullies had grown up. In fact, all three were now involved in anti-bullying groups in their communities, maybe trying to make up for their past actions. It was good to see that they'd come home to make amends...and that the community had embraced them.

"We have a table over there, if you guys want to sit with us," Bryce Witherspoon said, walking up to Isaac and Donna after they'd spent half an hour mingling. Isaac glanced over to where Bryce pointed and saw her brothers, Ry and Duke, their wives, Kaegan, Bryce's best friend Vashti and her husband Sawyer. Vaughn Miller, his sister, Zara, and Brody Dorsett - all former alums of their school - were also seated at the table.

Isaac glanced down at Donna. "You're ready to sit down?"

She nodded and glanced at her watch. "Yes, but I was hoping Nina would have arrived by now," she said. He tightened his grip on her hand and walked over to the table where the others were sitting.

"You want to call to see if she's okay?" he asked, after they'd greeted everyone at the table and while pulling Donna's chair out for her.

"I'll give her a few more minutes before worrying."

Although Isaac was certain Donna knew most of the people at the table, he wanted to make sure they all remembered her. Of course, they did. The only one who hadn't lived in the cove during their teen years had been Sawyer. He had moved to town a few years ago after being hired as the town's sheriff.

Vashti was expecting and the women were bombarding her with questions about the baby. Vashti beamed proudly over at her husband before announcing that she and Sawyer would be having another daughter. They already had twin girls in college, and a son who was barely two-years old.

Suddenly the entire room got quiet, and Isaac glanced around to determine why. Then he saw the reason—Nina Murray had arrived.

Chapter Seven

Donna fought back the tears that formed in her eyes. Nina stood at the entrance of the ballroom looking totally beautiful in a mango form-fitting dress that totally highlighted her figure. It was obvious some attendees had no idea who she was and were trying to figure out her identity. Others had figured it out, which accounted for the murmurs that suddenly began stirring around the room.

"Is that Nina Murray?" Ry asked.

Donna glanced over at him, smiling proudly. "Yes, that's Nina."

"She looks absolutely stunning," Ry's wife said and everyone at the table agreed.

Donna agreed as well. It wasn't just Nina's smaller size but also the outfit she'd chosen to wear. She looked absolutely amazing. However, Nina appeared nervous, as if she was contemplating turning around and leaving; not wanting to be the focus of everyone's attention after all. Donna understood and glanced over at Isaac. As if he comprehended her concerns, he nodded and said, "I'll go and let Nina know where we're sitting."

Then he stood and walked across the ballroom floor to Nina, leaning in and whispering something to her when he reached her. The smile that lit her face at that moment was striking. Nina took the arm Isaac presented to her as he escorted her over to the table while everyone in the room watched. Those who hadn't figured out Nina's identity before, knew who she was the moment she reached the table and Donna stood and engulfed her best friend in a huge hug.

"You look amazing, Nee," she whispered to her.

"Thanks," Nina said, finally taking a seat at the table after saying hello to everyone. Since she'd been born in Catalina Cove, like the majority of those seated at the table, the only person she didn't know was Sawyer. Introductions were made and conversations again started around the room. Several people came over to the table to say hello to Nina, including Rita, Monica and Faye.

Since Nina had missed the trio's apology, it was obvious she hadn't known what to expect when they approached. She was totally surprised when they apologized to her for their past behavior. Nina accepted their apology.

Afterwards, Alicia approached the table as if checking out her competition for the night. "Well Nina, I must say, you look good," Alicia said with a smile that didn't reach her eyes. "Who would have thought? How long do you plan to keep all the weight off? God knows there was a lot." Anyone knowing Alicia wasn't surprised that her compliment had been followed by an insult.

Donna took a sip of her drink. Poor Alicia. Evidently, she thought this was the same Nina who would cry when offended. Alicia was about to find out just how wrong that assumption was. "I've kept my weight off for more than ten years now, Alicia, and I don't see me gaining any back if I watch my diet and exercise regularly. What about you?"

Alicia lifted a brow. "What about me? I never had a weight problem."

"I wasn't referring to your weight," Nina said. "I was referring to your hair."

Alicia narrowed her eyes. "What about my hair?"

"It was thinning out years ago, but it looks fuller now. That transplant looks good."

Bam!

Several people at the table cleared their throats to keep from laughing. Donna watched as a deep frown covered Alicia's features. She had discovered, in an embarrassing way, that this Nina was not one to mess with and could give insults just like she got them...and she didn't mind doing so.

Without bothering to deny Nina's words, Alicia said, "I'd better get back to my table before the program starts." She then glanced over at Isaac. "Remember, we're hooking up while I'm in town," she said, as if to bolster her self-confidence once again.

"I'll be busy. Won't have any free time," Isaac replied with a serious look on his face.

Alicia smiled at him. "I heard you've retired, so I'm sure you'll be able to find time for me. And...you're now a free man, so there's no reason why you shouldn't." She then turned and walked off, deliberately swaying her hips as she did so.

"I see she hasn't changed," Vashti said, shaking her head. "Pushy as ever and still has you on her radar, Isaac."

"It's a waste of her time if she does," Isaac replied. He then glanced over at Donna and gave her a wink. She knew what that wink meant. In high school, that had been his way of letting Donna know he could handle Alicia. And he would.

His feelings about Alicia weren't really Donna's business, but he was making them her business. Ex or not, he wasn't about to let Alicia disrespect her. She appreciated that.

The room got quiet again when the mayor of Catalina Cove welcomed everyone and invited those who had moved away to think about coming back for good. He took a moment to tell them of all the great things going on in the cove, including a river taxi service to New Orleans that would eliminate highway traffic for those working in the city. That news got a round of applause.

Next came Reid Lacroix, the richest man in town. An earlier announcement stated tomorrow night's ice cream social was being sponsored by Mr. Lacroix, in memory of his late son Julius, who'd also been an alum under Principal Harding.

As an incentive to get people thinking about moving back to the cove, Mr. Lacroix offered low-interest loans to anyone who returned and wanted to bring their business with them. Of course, to retain the integrity of the town, it had to be a Catalina Cove approved business. A round of applause went out for that announcement as well.

The next person to speak was the man they'd all come to see. Donna thought Mr. Harding looked good for his age. So did Mrs. Harding, who'd been a math teacher.

After six years as principal at Catalina Cove High School, Mr. Harding had been offered a school superintendent position in Charlotte, North Carolina. The Hardings returned to the cove from time to time to visit and to go fishing, since Catalina Cove was well-known as the best place to throw out a fishing pole.

Dinner was served and Donna noticed how many men, who hadn't given Nina the time of day while in high school, were lining up to reserve a dance with her. Nobody asked Donna to dance, although they knew she was just as single as Nina. But with her ex-husband sitting there, and word circulating around the room that they were getting back together, none of the guys would have dared. Isaac had been pretty possessive back in high school. They probably figured nothing had changed.

"Would you dance with me, Donna?"

Donna glanced over at Isaac. Dinner had ended and the band had taken the stage. Couples were moving toward the dance floor. Arnett Staples, who'd been considered a bookworm in school and had been ridiculed as much as Nina, walked over to ask Nina to dance. Already, they were headed to the dance floor.

She glanced around and saw that the other couples at their table were on the floor dancing as well. Why did it have to be a slow number? She wasn't sure she was ready to be in Isaac's arms again. But then, she figured everyone would notice they were the only ones not dancing.

"Sure. I'd love to dance with you Isaac," she said, accepting the hand he offered. The band had begun playing another slow number, one that had been popular the year they'd graduated. It was a song Isaac and Donna had danced to plenty of times. He led her on the dance floor and the moment he pulled her into his arms, she felt it, the sense that this was where she belonged.

"This used to be our song," he whispered close to her ear, his voice strong, throaty and seductive.

Donna tipped her head back to glance up at Isaac and smiled. "Back in the day, every song used to be ours. Fast or slow, it didn't matter."

"Umm, but I liked the slow ones the best," he said, returning her smile.

Yes, you did, she thought, trying not to let him and his smile affect her. It was hard. The sheer power of his masculinity was overwhelming. "I bet you won't grind your body against mine like you did in the old days," he said, a taunting smile curving his lips.

Isaac and his smiles would be the death of her. "You're right. I won't."

He threw his head back and laughed. "Spoilsport."

She chuckled and their gazes met, causing full awareness to rip through her. Nothing had changed. It was pretty apparent that she and Isaac were still attracted to each other. But then, why wouldn't they be? They had dated all through high school and college and then spent nearly eight years together as a married couple. There was no way being in his arms would not influence her, wouldn't make her remember and wish for something that might have been.

Whether she liked it or not, Isaac was the only man she'd ever loved, the only man she'd ever wanted. She was one of those women who'd been ruined by the first man to claim her body, mind and soul. That was one of the reasons she hadn't bothered with dating anyone seriously after her divorce. Besides, she had felt no desire for anyone else. Other men had smiled at her, let their interest be known but they'd left her cold, not making her feel even a hint of yearning.

"What are you thinking about, Donna?"

She met his gaze. Could she tell him? Should she? She wanted to, but what good would it do? But still, she wanted to know how he'd spent his time without her. "I was just wondering what you've been doing over the past three years."

He shrugged those powerful shoulders. "That first year, I worked my ass off helping Uncle Mark. Hell, he had more energy than any man his age should have. I could barely keep up. A huge corporation wanted the microchip he created, and he was determined to have it ready by their deadline. The money they offered us, along with a percentage of controlling shares, made it possible for us to call it quits, take the money and enjoy life."

He paused a moment. "I was here less than six months and began wondering why I ever left. Why anyone ever left."

"You know why we all left, Isaac. To go off to college."

"But we didn't come back."

Donna nodded. "We had dreams to pursue."

"Yes, that's right. Dreams. I wonder how's that working out for everybody," he said, almost sarcastically.

She understood what he was saying. After all, they were a prime example. Their dreams had been to not only marry, but to stay together forever, make babies together, grow old together. So much for dreams. Instead of saying anything, she placed her head down on his chest as they swayed slowly to the music. She loved the feel of his hand slowly and gently caressing her back. Whether he knew it or not, his touch was playing havoc with her senses, causing mayhem to her mind and drugging her ability to think straight. For a short while, she wanted to pretend that they'd come here together as a married couple. That they'd managed to weather all their storms and lived their dreams. If only for a short while, she needed that pretense.

When the music ended, he took her hand and led her back to the table. She couldn't help wondering if he'd gotten as caught up in the moment as she had.

Everyone was excited about tomorrow's festivities. There would be a picnic at Lafitte Park, followed by the official lightning of the Christmas tree in the town's square that evening. That would be followed by an ice cream social in the school's auditorium. Before church on Sunday, compliments of Witherspoon Café, blueberry muffins and hot coffee would be served in the church's dining room. And after Sunday services, it would be dinner at Witherspoon Café for all.

Some would be leaving to catch flights after church and others, like Donna, would be flying out on Monday. A few like Nina and Alicia would hang around town for another week. Donna tried not to think about the moves Alicia intended to make on Isaac after she was gone. Isaac had tried to assure her that wouldn't be happening. Donna knew he could handle Alicia, the schoolgirl, but could he win against the fully grown-up, conceited and forever spoiled, yet still beautiful Alicia? The one who'd always wanted Isaac and now intended to get him?

"Ready to dance again?"

She glanced over at Isaac. Everyone was moving toward the dance floor to join in one of the line dances. She smiled over at him. "Sure."

He took her hand and led her toward the floor. She might as well enjoy every moment she could get with him. Monday would come soon enough.

Chapter Eight

"It's getting late and the crowd is starting to thin. I guess it's time to go," Donna said, sounding disappointed.

Isaac nodded. "Yes, I'm afraid you're right." But he wasn't ready for her to go her way and for him to go his.

He glanced at his watch. "It's not that late. You want to go somewhere for coffee?"

She looked up at him. "It's nearly two in the morning, Isaac. This is Catalina Cove. What place do you know that's still open at this hour?"

He held her gaze and said, "My place."

She sighed deeply. "I don't think that's a good idea."

He figured she would say that. "Can't blame a guy for trying. Come on, let me walk you to your car." He glanced around. "Where's Nina?"

"She left over an hour ago. I don't think she's ever danced that much, and she's probably exhausted."

He chuckled. "I noticed she was on the floor for almost every dance. Looks like she had fun."

Donna smiled. "She definitely made up for lost time. I'm happy for her."

"So am I."

They began walking out to the parking lot, side by side. It was a beautiful December night. The stars were shining bright in the sky, and a light breeze was chilling the air. When Isaac saw Donna shiver, he removed his jacket and placed it around her shoulders.

"Thank you, Isaac."

"Don't mention it."

It was on the tip of his tongue to tell her that nothing had changed, he would keep her safe from anything, even the elements of the universe, not to mention the Alicia Crawford's of the world. "Did you enjoy yourself tonight?"

"Yes, I did. I'm looking forward to tomorrow."

"Me, too." He wanted to see her again. Hell, he *needed* to see her again. He shoved his hands into his pockets as they continued walking. Isaac wasn't sure what he'd expected when he arrived tonight. Yes, he'd anticipated seeing his ex-wife, but he hadn't expected to recognize one particular thing. One very important thing.

He still loved her.

That realization had hit Isaac when he and Donna had danced together. More than anything, he wanted his wife back. The one thing giving him hope was that she was still using his name. She hadn't gone back to her maiden name, the way a lot of divorced women did. That had to mean something, didn't it? And just like he'd loved having her in his arms tonight, she'd clung to him too. It hadn't been hard to convince people that they were indeed getting back together. Most of their classmates who'd known just how madly in love they'd been in school saw their divorce as a temporary setback and nothing more.

"This is my car. At least, it's my rental," Donna said, breaking into his thoughts.

They came to a stop beside a dark blue sedan. He wasn't surprised. She always preferred a vehicle with four doors, while he always steered toward a two-seater. When he would tease her about it, Donna would say she was a mom-in-waiting. He wondered if she still thought about having children. His children.

"What hotel are you staying in?" he asked when she handed him back his jacket.

"There weren't any rooms available. But Nina's grandmother's house was empty, so she and I are staying there," she said. He opened the car door for her, and she got in.

He nodded, knowing exactly where the house was located. Nina's grandmother had been a wonderful lady and had always welcomed him. He couldn't count how many times he'd eaten dinner there with Nina and Donna. "Drive carefully and I'll see you tomorrow."

"Okay. Good night, Isaac. Thanks for everything. You made things easier for me tonight."

Had he? Deciding not to ask her to explain what she meant, he took a step away from the car. "Good night, Donna."

And then he watched as she drove away, his mind working up a plan to get his wife back.

"I can't believe you waited up for me," Donna said to Nina when she walked into the house and found her best friend sitting in front of a lit fireplace with a glass of wine. Another glass and the wine bottle were close by, letting Donna know Nina had been waiting on her.

"I wasn't sure you would be coming back here tonight," Nina said smiling. "Are the rumors true that were spreading around the ballroom tonight? Are you and Isaac getting back together?"

"You should know better than that, Nina," Donna said, kicking off her heels and sliding down on the sofa across from the fireplace.

"Then tell me what is true, Don," Nina said, pouring a glass of wine, then handing it to Donna.

Donna sighed deeply and took a sip of wine. "Okay, here goes." She told Nina all about Alicia's antics, and Isaac's plan to thwart her.

When she finished, Nina took a sip of her wine and said, "Why doesn't it surprise me that it all started with Alicia? She's been trying to get Isaac's attention forever. You guys might have started this to put Alicia in her place, but I think something happened tonight that the two of you hadn't counted on."

Donna took a sip of her wine again. "What?"

"You two were meant to be together. That was obvious tonight to anyone who saw the two of you together. The sexual chemistry radiating off both of you was too thick to even cut with a knife. And then when you danced...it was like you were the only two people on the dance floor. Hell, the only two people in the room."

Donna's pulse thickened as she remembered how Isaac had held her in his arms, their bodies pressed closed together as they slowly moved around the dance floor. She also remembered the lighthearted fun they'd had with others tonight. She'd felt comfortable being by his side. It was as if that was where she was supposed to be, and everybody there knew it...except for maybe Alicia.

She met Nina's gaze. "For a while there, I felt like we were the only ones in the room. I never realized how much I missed him, until tonight."

She'd also been aware of how much she'd missed being with him, having him hold her during the night while she slept, making love until she was too exhausted for anything other than sleep. She missed holding his hand and cuddling up on the sofa with him, watching television. She missed his closeness. The intimacy, that special physical and mental connection they'd always shared.

He hadn't kissed her goodbye tonight and she wondered why. Was it because with them, one kiss would have led to another and another? Those kisses would have broken her resolve and changed her mind about going to his home. She wasn't ready for that. Had he known it somehow? If so, then she appreciated him not taking advantage of her vulnerable state.

"Donna?"

She moved her gaze from the fire to Nina. "Yes?"

"What are you going to do about it?"

She shrugged her shoulders, as if in defeat. "There's nothing I can do, Nina. I'm the one who filed for divorce. Isaac will never forgive me."

Nina rolled her eyes. "Honestly, Donna. Did Isaac look like an angry man tonight? One short on forgiveness? To me, he looked like someone who would willingly give his wife another chance, if he thought she wanted it."

Donna's brain began scrambling. Would he? She knew they were attracted to each other, but then, a physical attraction was normal when you had as much history as they did. However, getting back together was something altogether different. It would be complicated. She still lived in Seattle and he was here in Catalina Cove. It was closer to Seattle than Boston, but still, there were thousands of miles between them. And she had no intention of leaving her job. Any attempt at another long-distance marriage was out of the question. They'd tried it once and it had failed. He would have no reason to believe she would do any better than she had the last time.

But still, what Nina said gave her something she'd thought she'd never have again with Isaac. Hope. "Do you really think so?"

Nina smiled and stared right at her, making sure their gazes were connected. It was something they'd done since they'd been kids, when they needed the other to believe what they were about to say. "Yes. Donna, I honestly believe that. But..."

Donna swallowed. "But what?"

"You'll have to be the one to make major changes. To ask him to do more would be unfair. You can't have things both ways. You know as well as I do that at some point, you need to decide."

"On what?"

"Who and what you love more—Isaac or your career."

Deciding it was time to change the subject, Donna said, "I noticed you and Arnett Staples hanging out in between dances." She noticed how bright Nina's eyes had gotten at the mention of Arnett's name.

"Arnett's an engineer working for NASA. He lives in Houston and is divorced. His ex-wife lives in D.C."

Donna nodded, taking another sip of her wine. "Did he tell you the reason for their breakup?"

"It was similar to your situation with Isaac. He had a solid job with NASA and she hated Texas and wanted to move back east to be close to her family. Therefore, she took a federal job in D.C."

Nina didn't say anything for a minute, then added, "So, I guess the career thing is a common problem for couples. I think that's sad when they can't compromise."

Donna thought about that for a moment, then asked, "Did he and his wife try to compromise?"

"He didn't say. But it's too late now—she married someone else."

Donna tried not to think about how she would feel if Isaac remarried. Although the subject hadn't come up between them, she didn't know for sure that he wasn't involved with someone, even if he had come to tonight's event alone. He hadn't kissed her goodbye. Was there a reason why not?

"He's nice."

Nina's words intruded into Donna's thoughts. "Who?"

"Arnett. That's who we were talking about, right?"

"Yes, of course," Donna said. "Arnett has always been a nice guy, just a bit of a nerd. He was more into books than girls or sports—not that there's anything wrong with that, mind you. He sure looks good without those thick eyeglasses."

Nina nodded. "He told me he'd had laser eye surgery. Who would have thought he was so good looking behind those eyeglasses? I guess it's the same with me. Who would have thought I looked fairly decent without all that weight? That just goes to show that people are more into what they see on the outside than what they can't see on the inside. Even Alicia tried making a play for Arnett tonight. Then again, she made a play for every single man there."

Donna had noticed but tried not to think about it. She knew that regardless of what Isaac had told Alicia earlier about being busy, the woman would still be stalking him the entire week she was in Catalina Cove.

"Is it true what you told Alicia about her hair?" Donna wanted to know.

Nina grinned. "Yes. I know the difference between a weave job and a transplant. What she does with her hair is her business, but I just wanted her to see that when you live in a glass house, you shouldn't throw stones. I also wanted to make sure she knew I wouldn't be putting up with her BS."

She then looked pointedly at Donna. "And don't think I don't know what you're doing by changing the subject. Admit it—you made a mistake by choosing a career over Isaac."

"I don't think that's what I did, Nina. I was trying to have them both and just went about it the wrong way." Donna took another sip of her wine. "Tonight, he told me about his first year in Boston, how he worked his ass off at his uncle's company. I hadn't known that. And even while working himself to death, he was still fighting hard for our weekends together. He didn't miss flying out to see me on his weekends in Seattle, not even once."

Nina nodded. "But if I recall, you missed flying out to be with him. Several times, in fact."

Donna sighed. Nina would remind her of that. "Yes, I did."

"So again, I have to ask you, Don. What do you want more—Isaac or your career?"

Chapter Nine

Isaac looked around the school's auditorium, where the ice cream social was being held. The planning committee had done an outstanding job with last night's and today's activities. From talking to a number of people, everyone had enjoyed the dance last night. The music had been awesome, with enough variety to satisfy everyone, and today's picnic had been great.

He had arrived at the auditorium early, since he'd promised Kaegan he would help set up some tables and chairs. But he'd known the moment Donna had arrived with Nina.

The moment their gazes connected, he felt intense desire that he only experienced with her. Sexual need ripped through him, making him pull in a deep breath before he could walk over to where she and Nina stood.

"Everything looks nice," Donna said glancing around.

"It sure does," Nina agreed.

Isaac nodded as he glanced around himself. It was either to do that, or just stand there and stare at Donna while thinking of all the naughty things he wanted to do to her. Some of them they'd done before, and he would love the chance to do again.

While glancing around, he had to admit, the place looked great. The room was decorated for the holidays, with candy canes hanging from the ceilings, and several huge snowmen strategically placed around the room. There was even a guy dressed as Santa Claus manning the table where the various ice cream toppings were located. And several ladies dressed as elves were serving.

He'd missed Christmas in Catalina Cove, and it seemed he wasn't the only one. It looked as if the committee had planned things that would bring back memories of how things used to be during the holidays.

The lighting of the Christmas tree earlier had been special because it wasn't just for the people at the holiday homecoming—all the residents of Catalina Cove had come. It had given those who'd returned home a chance to reunite with people they hadn't seen in years, and to catch up on what had happened since they'd left.

Isaac had overheard numerous former classmates say that they were contemplating moving back. They hadn't realized what a great place Catalina Cove was until after they'd left. It was a warm and friendly community that consisted of people who cared for each other. Those who lived in big cities talked about liking the lack of traffic but what they missed more than anything was the ocean. And they all admitted that Reid Lacroix's offer of a low-interest small business loan was a good incentive to move back.

"I see Arnett standing over there. I'll see you guys later," Nina said before walking off and leaving them alone.

Isaac glanced back at Donna, thinking about how good she looked in her long flowing skirt and tunic blouse. There'd been a four-hour rest period after the lighting of the Christmas tree and now everyone had returned looking refreshed and ready to hang out and socialize while eating ice cream. There were numerous serving stations set up so lines could move quickly. "Ready for a bowl of ice cream, Donna?"

She lifted a brow. "Just a bowl?"

He threw his head back and laughed, immediately remembering how much she loved ice cream. She had no particular favorite flavor of ice cream; she could eat it at any time of year. It could be freezing cold outside and Donna would be sitting in front of the fireplace, eating ice cream. A trip to the ice cream shop had always been one sure-fire way to get him out the doghouse. "Sweetheart, you can have as much ice cream you want. Looks like there's plenty."

Too late, he realized his term of endearment. *Sweetheart.* Calling her that had been natural and sounded right. Although she didn't say anything, he knew she'd been aware of what he'd said as well. They walked over to one of the servers, Vashti Alcindor Grisham, and ordered. He got one scoop, but Donna asked Vashti to load her up.

"I see you're still an ice cream addict," Vashti said, laughing.

Most of Catalina Cove knew of Donna's love for ice cream. She would be waiting on the Hamptons to open their ice cream shop every Saturday morning, and would drop in again before they closed Saturday evening.

"Yes, totally," Donna said.

"Yes, totally," Isaac agreed too, grinning.

Vashti laughed. Then she said in a thoughtful tone, "After the Hamptons passed away, no one wanted to keep the ice cream shop open. Everyone became satisfied with just buying ice cream from the grocery stores, but it wasn't the same. That ice cream shop did more than sell ice cream. It was a place we could hang out and have fun."

Donna remembered, smiling. "Remember how they would make a big production of it when a new flavor came out? And we would all have to taste it to see if it was worthy of being served at the Hampton's Ice Cream Shop?"

Vashti grinned. "I also remember you being first in line at all the tastings."

Donna nodded, laughing. "I most certainly was."

Moments later, Donna and Isaac nodded to Vashti and moved on to look at the school pictures on the wall. The committee had put up all the yearbook pictures as well as a few they'd found in the school's library. They'd even made a video, and everyone gathered around the huge screen to watch as someone dimmed the lights. Isaac wasn't surprised to see how often he and Donna had appeared together onscreen.

There had also been sad moments—when they'd seen some of their former classmates who were no longer with them.

"I can't believe how many times we appeared together in that video," Donna said, grinning over at Isaac when the lights came back on.

"We were quite a team then," he said, hoping it would give her something to think about.

At that moment, someone suggest a game of cards and teams were set up. Of course, Donna and Isaac were on the same team. A few hours later, their team had won, and each member was given a bag of Christmas candy.

As everyone filed out of the school's auditorium at midnight, a lot of people admitted that they were sorry the night was over. Someone suggested driving over to New Orleans to hit a few nightclubs, saying that they could make it to church in the morning, though they might sleep through the sermon. Isaac couldn't wait to see how that worked out. Would the ushers come nudge them awake, like they did in the good old days?

While some of the others left, Donna was in the process of finishing off one last ice cream cone. Every time she licked the damn thing, Isaac had to remind himself to breathe. He remembered just how well she'd use that same tongue to lick him. More than once, he shifted in his chair to ease the tightness behind his zipper.

"Since Nina is joining the group going to New Orleans, do you need a ride back to her grandmother's place?" he asked, hoping talking would take his mind off what Donna was doing with her tongue.

She met his gaze. "Yes. Nina offered to leave me the car, but I figured it would be better if she took it. If she caught a ride with someone, she wouldn't be able to come home when she wanted to. Do you mind dropping me off?"

"It would be my pleasure."

"Hey Elloran and Elloran. You two spending the night here?" a classmate who was taking down holiday decorations jokingly called out.

"We're on our way," Isaac called back, laughing. When he returned his gaze to Donna, he saw she had finished her cone. "Ready to go?"

She nodded. "Yes, I'm ready."

They had barely pulled out of the school's parking lot when Donna heard Isaac say her name. She recognized that tone and knew what she would see when she glanced over at him. She met his dark eyes and immediately felt sexual awareness sweep through every part of her body. It was there, even in the very air she was breathing. But it hadn't just appeared. That awareness had been there all night, and even before that. He had been by her side all through the day, and she'd been conscious of every move he made.

Being around Isaac today had again made her realize how much she'd missed him...and how attracted she still was to him. How attracted they were to each other. The chemistry between them could always be sparked to life by a touch, a look, even a scent. It had never taken much to make them hungry for each other. And it seemed nothing had changed.

There had never been a time she hadn't desired her husband. She and Isaac had enjoyed a great life, in and out of the bedroom. But she had *definitely* enjoyed the times she'd spent in the bedroom with him.

When he said her name again, she answered. "Yes?"

"I'd rather take you to my place, instead of Nina's grandmother's house."

He had mentioned taking her to his place last night and she'd refused. Why was he bringing it up again tonight? "Why?"

He smiled and a part of her wished he hadn't. When he smiled like that, desire—hot and sharp—made her stomach clench.

"Aren't you curious, Donna?"

She swallowed deeply. "About what?"

"Whether I'm still a slob."

Donna couldn't help but laugh. "You were never a slob, Isaac. You just weren't the tidiest person in the world. I hope that has changed."

"It has. But don't you want to see for yourself?"

Did she? She knew she shouldn't. Not when just being around him had desire and need coiling within her very core. He'd always seemed to know when she wanted him. Could he sense that now?

"I'm not sure going to your place is a good idea."

"You said that last night. What's wrong? When you get there, do you think I'll offer you more than coffee?"

Donna lifted a brow. She knew Isaac. "Wouldn't you?"

A huge smile touched his lips. "Yes, I would. But you don't have to take it."

Yeah. Right. Like she could resist him. When it came to Isaac, she had no willpower. But now, she saw the opportunity to ask him something she'd been curious about since getting the invitation. "Are you seeing anyone?"

He brought the car to stop at a traffic light and met her gaze. "No."

She nibbled on her bottom lip. "Then why didn't you kiss me last night?" She'd told herself she wouldn't ask him. Although she'd had her own ideas, she had to hear the real reason from him.

He pulled his car off the road into the lot of a closed gas station. Killing the engine, he turned to her. "I haven't seen or talked to you in almost three years, Donna. I never changed my phone number on you, but you changed yours on me. I sent you Christmas cards that you never acknowledged and I, of all people, know how much you—"

"You sent me Christmas cards?" she interrupted to ask.

"Yes. Every year but this one. I figured you didn't want them, so I decided to stop sending them."

"I never saw them."

"Well, I sent them. I knew our address and since they didn't return to me, I had no reason to believe you hadn't gotten them."

How could she explain that she'd stopped opening any Christmas cards that came her way? Seeing the cards, and knowing others were enjoying the holidays when she wasn't, just depressed her more.

"I don't open Christmas cards, Isaac. Not just yours but anyone's. I don't even take the time to see who sent them."

He frowned. "Why?"

She shrugged, deciding to be honest. "After you left, Christmas wasn't the same anymore."

He didn't say anything for a moment, then admitted, "I didn't know that." "Why did you change your phone number?"

Now that reason was a real weird one. "Because I started getting crazy phone calls. It started with a wrong number. Then the guy said he liked the way I sounded and wanted to talk to me more often. I told him that I preferred that he didn't. He started calling me anyway and became quite a nuisance. I became afraid that somehow, he would find out where I lived. Finally, I complained to the police. They told me all I could do was change my number, so I did. I never thought you would want to stay in touch."

"I wanted to check on you to see how you were doing. But when you changed your phone number and didn't acknowledge my Christmas cards, I figured you didn't want the contact. So, I made a promise to myself that if we ever saw each other again, it would be up to you to make the first move."

He then turned back around and started the car again. Before putting it in gear, he asked her, "So, is it Nina's grandmother's house or mine?"

Donna didn't say anything for a minute as she absorbed his words. He had wanted to stay in touch with her because he'd cared about how she was doing. And he had tried calling her and had sent her Christmas cards. She hadn't known. He was close to her parents and she'd known he had stayed in contact with them. But foolish her, had made them promise not to bring up Isaac whenever they talked. Chances were, they knew that he'd made millions on his business and had moved back to Catalina Cove.

Drawing in a deep breath, knowing the full extent of what she was doing, she said. "Take me to your place, Isaac."

Chapter Ten

"So, what should I expect when I get to your home?" Isaac glanced over at Donna and smiled before returning his eyes to the road. "A tidy house for one thing."

"And what's number two?" she asked him.

He knew he had to be honest—there was no way he could lie. Not when his body was hard for her. And just like he could always tell when she wanted him, she had the ability to tell when he wanted her. "Whatever you want. Like I said, it's your move, Donna."

"And if I make that move?"

"Then I can guarantee that you won't regret it."

They'd always been at their best in bed. She was the only woman whose touch could have him out of his mind with desire, who could practically make him explode just from inhaling her feminine scent. "And," he decided to add, "You can spend the night if you'd like." Little did she know, he intended to give her every reason to want to.

"And if I did, Isaac, what would happen tomorrow?"

"Whatever you want. There's been no other woman in my life since you." He brought his car to a stop in front of a huge gate. "Welcome to my home."

She glanced out the front windshield and a huge smile touched her lips. She then looked back at him with surprise in her eyes. "You bought it! You actually bought it."

His smile matched hers. "Yeah, I did. Old man Landrum died without heirs, so the state put it up for sale right after I moved here."

When they'd been teenagers, the Landrum Estate was the house they'd talked about owning one day. Of course, it had been a dream since they never imagined having enough money to buy it. Isaac would never forget the day he'd signed the papers. The huge ocean-front house that sat on five acres, with a majestic landscaped lawn and surrounded by a huge wrought iron gate, was to have been his and Donna's dream home. He'd wished she could have been with him when he'd made the purchase.

"It's beautiful, Isaac."

"Thanks." He used his car's remote to open the security gates. "There's still a lot of work to be done. Over the last few years, Landrum let the place go because of his health. I live in the downstairs part of the house while work is being done in the upper part."

He brought the car to a stop in the horseshoe-shaped driveway. After turning off the ignition, he quickly opened the vehicle's door and walk around to the other side to open her door.

"Thanks."

After assisting her out the vehicle, he took her hand and led her to the huge double door. He opened it and stood back as she crossed over the threshold.

Following her inside, he said, "Let me get the lights."

He flipped the switch on the lights, and Donna glanced around in awe. It was obvious he'd kept most of the original furniture—it was early American style and it fit the decor of the house. She loved the huge fireplace and the mantel over it. Although she'd never been inside the Landrum home, she had heard that back in the day, it had been one of the most elegant homes in the cove.

And Isaac had bought it.

She turned to find him staring at her. He had removed his leather jacket and stood there, looking the epitome of sexy. "Well, what do you think?" he asked.

Donna knew he was referring to this place, but all her thoughts were on him when she said, "Beautiful."

She knew men didn't consider themselves as beautiful, but she thought the one standing across the room was. Just looking at him made her body throb in places it hadn't throbbed in nearly three years.

"Tidy enough for you?" he asked grinning.

She chuckled. "Neat as a pin."

As they continued to look into each other's eyes, amusement was replaced with desire. She knew exactly why she was here tonight. For him, it might only be about sex, but for her, it was more. They had once loved each other in ways others had never fully understood. Isaac had been her life. Her soulmate. Her very reason for living. Yet she had driven him away.

At that moment, she again reaffirmed in her heart that she still loved him and had made a grave mistake in letting him go.

She glanced around again. "Why did you buy this house, Isaac?"

He shoved his hands into the pockets of his jeans. It was a gesture he did whenever he was serious about something. "I bought it because I wanted it. I've always wanted to live here, even when I was too poor to even consider such a thing. But then that's what dreams are for, right? To think the impossible might one day come true."

He paused a moment and then said, "Remember how we would walk by here on our way to school? How we would peer through the gate and imagine ourselves living here? When I saw that wasn't going to be a possibility, I decided to fulfil my dream alone."

There was nothing Donna could say, except... "I am happy for you." Yes, she was happy for him, but sad for herself. He had reached his dreams without her. He'd managed to retire at thirty-four...even though that had never been part of the dream. They figured unless they won lottery, they would be working well into their fifties, possibly sixties; especially if they had kids to put through college. Early retirement had been too much to hope for. But Isaac had done it.

And he had their house. *Their* house. Now it was his house. A part of her wanted to break down and cry but she knew she couldn't. It was her own fault her dreams hadn't come true.

He'd said that she would have to make the first move and she could tell from the look in his eyes that he was waiting for her to make it. Acting on adrenaline of the most potent kind, she slowly crossed the room to where he stood. A part of her needed to know his intentions—did he just want to get her naked? But what if he asked her about getting back together? She didn't have an answer for that. He lived here now, and she couldn't ask him to move back to Seattle? And as much as she would love to, she couldn't move here. There was still no middle ground for them. In essence, nothing had changed. As much as she loved him, all they would have is whatever time they spent together while she was here in the cove. On Monday, she would be flying back to Seattle, as planned.

"Just so you know, Isaac," she said, when she came to a stop in front of him. "No other man has shared my life since you. Seriously or otherwise."

There she'd said it. She'd basically told him she had not slept with another man since him. There hadn't been anyone she had wanted to share her bed or her body with. She recognized the intense look that immediately appeared in his eyes. The sensual heat that darkened them even more. If they slept together tonight, they would make up for lost time. Or die trying. Is that what she wanted? Evidently, since she had come here knowing full well what to expect.

"Would you like something to drink, Donna?"

She shook her head. "No, I don't think so." She took a step closer to him.

No one could ever accuse Isaac of being slow and Donna wasn't surprised when he asked, "Are you making your move, Donna?"

She nodded. "That's what I'm doing, Isaac." Every word made a tingle of anticipation stir in her stomach.

"What if I were to tell you that I intend to make up for lost time?" he said, removing her jacket and tossing it aside.

"Then I would say, bring it on."

The chemistry between them was explosive and Donna had a feeling they both felt it. The look in his eyes was sending sensual shivers through her bones, urging her to surrender to the sexual needs within her. Needs that hadn't been taken care of in a long time.

She watched his gaze drop from her eyes to scan her outfit. "I like what you're wearing, by the way."

"I like your clothes, too. But I'd like you better out of them," she said, as she reached up to unbutton his shirt. More than anything, she needed to rub her hands across his bare chest, to feel the warmth of his skin, to let his chest hair trickle through her fingers, and to bury her face in his shoulder. She had missed those things.

His hands were busy as well. She'd worn her hair up and he was reaching around to remove the tie, allowing her hair to fall in soft waves around her shoulders. He'd always preferred her to wear her hair down.

"Hmm, just the way I like it," he said smiling.

"And just what I needed to feel," she said, running her fingers through the hair on his chest.

"Now for the main attraction," he said, leaning in to claim her mouth. It was so familiar, so very, *very* good, Donna almost forgot to breathe.

But she knew what was coming next. How Isaac wouldn't just kiss her but would make love to her mouth. He would start off by devouring her tongue, making it a slave to his wants, needs, and desires. He was a master, using his tongue to ignite sensations of pleasure with every stroke.

Like it was doing now.

His mouth was taking hers with a degree of possession that surged through her body with bone-melting fire. She often wondered how he managed to do this. Use his tongue, as well as his lips to suck, lick, and tease her into a moaning, shuddering surrender. All her pent-up desires from the past three years were being pulled out of her. This kiss seemed to reach into her very soul.

With toe-curling determination, she kissed him back, wanting to put into action what she was too scared to say, too embarrass to admit. She had dreamed about him every night. She'd even name her battery-operated toy after him, even though it hadn't come close in the satisfaction department. But something was better than nothing. Still, this experience right here made her realize that nothing came close to being with Isaac.

He suddenly released her mouth. "I love the taste of you, Donna. I can't get enough."

Then before she could utter a single word, he quickly dropped to his knees, tugged down her skirt, along with her panties, leaned in and latched his mouth to her sex. He proceeded to suck her clit into his mouth, nipped at it, then closed his mouth firmly over it while letting his tongue delve deep inside of her.

Donna grabbed hold of Isaac's shoulders as he seduced her sex with hot, deep glides of his tongue. Fire moved through her veins as everything inside of her awakened. Intense need consumed her. She needed more, more... Almost there... And with a final stroke of Isaac's tongue, she screamed herself to an orgasm.

Isaac swept Donna into his arms and moved quickly to his bedroom. He had to get inside of her now. He'd never been with a woman like Donna. Just a taste of her had him hard as a rock.

He placed her on the bed and practically tore off his clothes. He was about to reach for a condom when she said, "That's not necessary, Isaac. I want to feel all of you. I *need* to feel all of you. Skin-to-skin. I'm still on the pill and I'm safe."

Her words caused need to thicken his blood. "I'm safe, too. And more than anything in this world, I want to be skin-to-skin with you, too, sweetheart," he said, tossing the condom packet aside. Then he returned to the bed, intent on removing the rest of her clothing.

He had dreamed of this moment, though he'd honestly thought it would never happen. But it was happening. She was here, in his home, in his bed. And not only was he about to make love to her, but he intended to possess her in the most primal way a man could take the woman he loved. And he did love her. He always had and always would.

He got on the bed, straddling her body. Staring down at her breasts, he whispered, "Beautiful," before lowering his head and swiping over her nipples with his tongue.

"Isaac..."

Hearing her say his name made heat curl inside of him. Made him eager to get inside of her.

"Open your eyes and look at me, Donna."

She lifted eyelids that had been covering desire-filled eyes. He looked down at her, meeting her gaze, then he thrust hard into her, buying himself inside as far as humanly possible to go. Then he began riding her, just the way she'd always liked. Moving in and out with deep, powerful strokes. And she moved with him—pure sensuous energy beneath him. Her fingers dug in his shoulders, but he didn't mind. Nor did he mind when her legs wrapped tight around him.

His body was on fire and his shaft was throbbing inside of her, begging for release. He held back, determined to make their lovemaking last as long as he could. He moaned when he felt her inner muscles tighten around him, trying to pull everything out of him, practically demanding what he was fighting to hold back.

Isaac wasn't sure how long he could last, but he would try. For her.

Sensations were assaulting Donna at every angle. Isaac's body was hammering into hers, making heat flood her insides and liquid fire pool in her belly. The thickness of his erection had stretched her and was whipping her into a pleasure frenzy of the most erotic kind. Her breasts were tingling and the area where their bodies were joined was on fire. Suddenly, he shifted slightly, and her heart slammed in anticipation because she knew what he was doing. He was aiming for her g-spot. And he knew exactly where it was.

The moment he hit it, her body splintered into a million spasms, and she screamed his name for the second time that night. Suddenly, she felt his body jerk and he threw his head back at the same time he exploded, filling her to the core with his essence. She could feel him flood her insides, igniting electrical currents everywhere it flowed.

Every emotion she could name filled her, but the one that mattered most was love. She loved this, she loved him, she loved them. His hips continued to rock against her, preparing her body for another round. Multiple orgasms were common with them and she had a feeling he intended for them to make love well into the next day. Or die trying. But what a way to go.

Chapter Eleven

Donna felt daylight on her face but refused to open her eyes. If this was a dream, she wasn't ready to wake up. She had been made love to. Thoroughly. Totally. All through the night. And she'd been held in strong arms while she slept.

Just like old times.

"Are you going to wake up now or not?"

She refused to open her eyes, but the sound of that deep, husky voice made her smile. She couldn't help herself. The man was something else. "And if I don't?" she said, her eyes still closed.

"I have ways of waking you up."

Her smile widened even more as she remembered some of those ways. Naughty ways. On second thought, maybe she shouldn't open her eyes. "Do you really want me to open my eyes, Isaac?"

"It's your call, sweetheart."

Grudgingly, she opened her eyes to find Isaac right there, his face close to hers. "Good morning, Isaac."

"And it is a good morning, sweetheart." He kissed her and by the time their mouths separated, she had to agree—it was the best morning she'd had in three years.

"I hope Nina's not worried about you."

Donna cuddled closer to him. "She's not. I text her earlier to let her know I was with you. Besides, she has an overnight guest, so I won't be missed."

"Who?"

"Arnett."

Isaac smiled. "Good for him. He used to have a serious crush on her in high school."

Donna blinked. "I didn't know that. I thought the only thing he was interested in was geometry, calculus, and physics."

"Yeah, he had it bad for her. His locker was next to mine, and I remember finding a letter he'd written to her. It had fallen out of his backpack."

"You never told me that, Isaac."

"Guys don't talk about that kind of thing. Besides, I figured that if Nina had gotten the letter, she would have mentioned it to you, and you would have told me. Because she never did, I figured he'd changed his mind about giving it to her."

"Yes, but had you told me, they could have—"

He captured her mouth in his and the moment he slid his tongue inside, she released a moan that fired her lower extremities. She'd thought she'd never experience this again. His taste. His smell. His lovemaking.

He slowly released her mouth, then looked into her eyes. At that moment, she knew they were both thinking the same thing—how had they turned their backs on this? But then, he hadn't turned his back on it. She had.

"Let it go for now, Donna."

His words proved she'd been right. "I'm not sure if I can, Isaac." There was no need to admit that she'd messed up when she didn't have any idea about how to make things better. Make-up sex had always been fantastic between them, but they usually did it *after* finding a solution to their problem. Right now, there was no solution in sight.

"Then let me show you how to let it go." And he captured her mouth again.

After church, those who didn't have a flight to catch headed over to the Witherspoon Café for Sunday dinner. The place was crowded, and everyone agreed that the food was even better than they remembered. Tables had been rearranged to accommodate the large crowd, and someone remarked it felt like they were back in the school's cafeteria... although nobody recalled the food being this good.

After dinner there were hugs, teary goodbyes, and promises of doing a better job of staying in touch. Someone even mentioned it would be a great idea to do this every year and the masses all agreed. The planning committee had again thanked everyone for coming and encouraged everyone to respond to the surveys that would follow.

Isaac walked Donna back to his car to leave the café. He had to admit, he felt...happy, in a way he hadn't felt in a long time. This was how it was meant to be. His mind went back to that morning. After making love a few more times, he had taken Donna back to Nina's grandmother's house so she could get dressed for church. When they walked in, Arnett and Nina had been sitting at the kitchen table eating breakfast and had invited them to join them. Isaac remembered what a great cook Nina's grandmother had been, and she had undoubtedly passed that skill on to her granddaughter, because breakfast had been delicious. All in all, it had been a *very* good morning.

"I can't believe what happened to Bryce," Donna said, interrupting his thoughts. "That she had gotten kidnapped."

Bryce had told everyone at dinner about her narrow escape from a serial killer a couple of months ago, listing it as one of the few Catalina Cove misadventures. "And I agree with what Bryce said, Isaac. You're a hero, right along with Kaegan."

He shook his head. "My part wasn't a big deal."

She pushed against him teasingly. "Your part *was* a big deal. If you hadn't installed all that security equipment on Eagle Bend Inlet, Kaegan would never have known that someone was trespassing on his property."

Isaac didn't want to think of what Bryce's fate might have been if Kaegan hadn't been alerted and acted. "It was Kaegan's idea to install the equipment in the first place. I'm just glad things turned out and Bryce was okay."

"Me, too. Nothing exciting ever happened in Catalina Cove while I was living here."

"The cove can do without that kind of excitement, trust me. Since the guy pleaded guilty to killing a number of women, he was put away for a long time," Isaac said, opening the car door for Donna.

After walking around and getting in on the other side, he looked over at her. "What time do you fly out tomorrow?"

"At eleven in the morning."

He nodded. Although tempted, he refused to ask her to stay. He'd learned his lesson about trying to compete with her work. During their time together, neither one had talked about what might happen after this weekend. And now that she was leaving tomorrow, he figured that she considered this weekend one and done. She'd had her sexual fix and was probably good for a while. His stomach hurt, just thinking about it.

"So, where would you like to go now?" he asked her before starting the car.

She smiled over at him. "I have an idea. Would you drop me off at Nina's so I can pack? Then I'll drive my rental over to your place, and if you don't mind, I'll stay the night again. I can head out to the airport in the morning from your house."

"Of course, I don't mind." He smiled, happy that she didn't seem to want to leave him just yet. It was a start.

"I'm glad you're spending your last hours in Catalina Cove with Isaac, Donna."

Donna glanced over at Nina and smiled. "Are you happy because I'm out the way, so you can enjoy Arnett? I heard him mention to Isaac that he's staying in the cove for another week as well. Imagine that?"

A huge grin appeared on Nina's face. "I am imagining it. Trust me. In fact, you don't want to know just what all I'm imagining."

Donna couldn't help but laugh. It had been a long time since she'd seen Nina act so giddy over a guy. "I can tell you really like him."

A serious expression appeared on Nina's face. "Yes, I do. I know it's been a long time since we really knew each other, but we have a lot in common." She paused a minute and then added, "He even claims he liked me back when we were in school, but I'm not sure I should believe him."

"Believe him because it's true."

Nina stared at her, surprised. "And how do you know that?"

"Isaac told me last night. He and Arnett had lockers beside each other. One day Arnett dropped a letter and Isaac picked it up. It was addressed to you. Isaac gave it back."

Nina thought for a minute, then said, "He told me that he used to write me letters all the time but was too afraid to give them to me. I never knew."

Donna reached out and took her friend's hand. "Now you do. What are you going to do about it?"

Nina smiled. "In case you haven't been paying attention, Donna, I'm already doing something about it. We have agreed to continue to see each other this week, and we'll stay in touch after we both go home. I even invited him to visit me in California for Christmas."

Donna lifted a brow. "I guess I'm getting kicked to the curb for the holidays then. I thought you were coming to Seattle to spend Christmas with me."

"Oops. I figured with you and Isaac trying to work things out that the two of you would be spending Christmas together."

Donna didn't say anything. The pause in conversation was obviously too long for Nina, who asked, "The two of you are working things out, right?"

Knowing Nina would bug her until she got an answer she said, "We haven't talked about anything."

Nina lifted a brow. "What have the two of you been doing? Wait! Don't answer that." Leaning back against the sofa, Nina asked. "Don't you think at some point the two of you should call a time-out and talk about it?"

"Yes, but..."

"But nothing. What are you afraid of?"

Donna tilted her head back and glanced up at the ceiling for a few seconds. She then looked back at Nina. "Rejection. I hurt him. He will never want me back in his life. I'm not even sure I deserve to be back in his life. He has it all, Nina. He has everything I could be sharing with him, if only I had believed in him. If only I hadn't put my career ahead of him. If only I—"

"I get that, Donna. But maybe he still loves you and is willing to give you another chance."

"But that's just it. Nothing has changed. I still live and work in Seattle and he's here."

"And you're not willing to compromise, are you?"

Donna nibbled on her bottom lip. "I love my job."

Nina rolled her eyes. "Yes, and they love you back so much that they passed you over on that last promotion. A promotion you deserved," she said, reminding Donna of what she'd finally gotten around to telling Nina a few weeks ago. "When are you going to wake up and realize that your job is not going to keep you warm at night, and likely won't even make you happy for much longer? You better believe if Arnett even hinted that he wanted me to move to Texas, I would be on the next plane with a cowgirl outfit on."

"Yes, but you'd be able to get a job at any hospital. There's only one Cohen Advertising Agency."

"And there's only one Isaac Elloran."

And there's only one Isaac Elloran.

Nina's words raced through Donna's mind as she drove to Isaac's house. She was already dreading leaving Catalina Cove. She'd miss the town but more importantly, she would miss Isaac.

There wasn't anyone quite like him. She'd always known it. He had been different from the other guys she'd known in school. He was very good-looking, but also kind, considerate and respectful. Everybody liked him—they couldn't help themselves.

And he'd been loved by her.

He still was.

The moment her car reached the huge wrought iron gate, it automatically opened for her and she drove through to the horseshoe driveway. The door opened and Isaac came out of the house dressed differently than he had been earlier. They had gone straight to the café from church, so he'd been dressed up. But now, he had removed his suit and was wearing a pair of jeans and a pull-over sweater.

"I thought maybe you'd changed your mind," he said when she got out of the car.

"Saying goodbye to Nina took longer than I thought it would," she said, going to the trunk to get her luggage. There was no need to tell him just what she and Nina had talked about for so long.

"I'll get this," he said, coming to take the luggage from her. "I see you still don't travel light."

She smiled over at him as they walked together toward his door. "Is there any woman who can?"

He chuckled. "I think that somewhere in this universe there might be."

As soon as they were inside, he closed the door and placed her luggage on the floor, then pulled her into his arms. "I missed you."

She smiled. "I wasn't gone that long."

"Long enough."

He then swept her off her feet and carried her into the bedroom.

Chapter Twelve

Isaac eased out of bed while Donna slept. In less than four hours, she would be out of his life again, and he wasn't sure how he was going to handle that. They had spent the weekend together, yet neither of them had made any promises. In fact, they hadn't even discussed their lives beyond this weekend. Sure, they'd made up for lost time physically, but hadn't given any consideration as to how it would affect them mentally once they were apart again.

He knew how it would affect him.

Sliding into his jogging pants and putting on a hoodie and running shoes, he left the room. Before leaving for his early morning jog, he rekindled the blaze in the fireplace. Temperatures in the cove didn't usually dip below fifty this time of year, but forecasters were predicting a cold front to move in, and the next two days, the temperatures could get as low as thirty-five. Still, he would rather be here than back in Boston or Seattle. Catalina Cove was the place for him and a part of him wished there was some way that Donna would feel the same way.

Throughout the weekend, the only time she mentioned her job was that one time he'd asked her about it. He was sure she still loved it. And now that she was single, her travels wouldn't be limited. She was an ambitious woman who was moving up the corporate ladder, with nothing—and nobody—holding her back.

But she had admitted that Christmas wasn't the same for her without him. Should that give him hope? For a little while it had, but since she hadn't mentioned it again, that hope had pretty much fizzled out.

As he left the house, he tried to push away the thought that he might have hindered her career goals. He didn't think so—he had bent over backwards to support her—but maybe she hadn't seen it that way.

He glanced around and breathed in the fresh December air. One of the things he loved more than anything about his home was its beach access. There was nothing better than having the ocean right in his back yard. He looked out toward the water and saw that there were already a number of boats out there. High temperatures or low temperatures, no matter the day of the week, nothing could keep the fishermen off the waters surrounding the cove and he understood. In Catalina Cove, owning a boat was second nature. It was like owning a bicycle. Isaac had lived for the days when his dad, Isaac Elloran Sr., would put work aside to spend a day out in his small boat with his son.

Jogging at a moderate pace, his feet pounded the beach sand while uncertainty pounded his heart. He knew he still loved Donna—that wasn't the issue. But what he didn't know was how she felt about him. She had admitted she had not slept with anyone since their divorce, so maybe for her, this weekend might have been nothing more than a chance to take the edge off. He and Donna had always enjoyed a vigorous sex life, so for her to go without sex... Well, that had probably put her in a bad way. They had made love for most of the weekend. And he had been more than glad to accommodate her; however, he didn't just want to take care of her physical needs. He wanted to be what she needed—body and soul.

There was a time when he'd felt that he had been. What had happened to change that? It no longer mattered to him what went wrong in their marriage. What was important now was figuring out how to fix it. But how could they do that when nothing was resolved. He had tolerated living in Boston, but he loved returning to Catalina Cove. Being back made him realize just how lucky he'd been to grow up in a town with such loving and caring people. No matter how long people were away from the cove, when they returned, the town welcomed them back because they belonged to it.

Isaac knew Donna had enjoyed being home this weekend—she'd told him. But had she enjoyed it enough to ever contemplate moving back for good? Or was her job all she still cared about. Was her dream of becoming Advertising Director of one of the largest advertising firms in the country the only thing that was important to her?

He continued jogging, picking up the pace as he sprinted across the thick sand. He was looking at another Christmas without her, and he honestly didn't know how he was going to deal with it. He loved his wife and wanted her back. But was he willing to give up everything here to satisfy what she wanted? If he did, would he grow to resent her? And why was he still willing to bend over backwards for her, when she hadn't done it for him?

He knew the answer. Because he loved her. But then, since she wasn't willing to do the same for him, did that mean that she didn't love him...at least, not to the same degree?

He didn't want to waste his last hours with her feeling frustrated or resentful. However, they did need to at least talk about this weekend, to see if it was something they could build on. For all he knew, she might like being a divorcee; a single woman, accountable to no one but herself. Hell, he didn't know if she even still wanted children. At church, Donna had met Ray Sullivan and his wife Ashley. He'd watched how Donna had interacted with their twin babies, saying how adorable they were. When he'd told her about how Ray had lost his memory and he and his wife had found each other, she had made the comment that some people were meant to be together, no matter what. Had she been hinting that the same thing applied to them?

Unfortunately, although she'd told him how much she'd enjoyed their lovemaking, she hadn't given him any reason to think she still loved him. Come eleven that morning, she would get on a plane and go back to Seattle...taking his heart with her, like she'd always done.

Isaac had known not to get his hopes up when it came to Donna. When duty called, she would leave him at the drop of a hat. He thought of the countless times she'd rushed out in the middle of dinner because of some screw-up at the office that she had to take care of. It had always been one important project after another for her, as if she was the only one in the company capable of fixing things. And he honestly believed she thought she was.

Sharing the weekend with her had been amazing, but he refused to let her leave without knowing just where he stood with her. If she said nowhere, then he'd know it was time to finally move on with his life. He couldn't continue to live like this. When he got back home, he would broach the subject with her—whether she wanted to talk about it or not.

Donna woke up to find herself alone in Isaac's big bed. He'd mentioned he jogged on the beach at six every morning, so that's probably where he had gone. They used to jog each morning together, but since he hadn't invited her to join him, she figured he needed some time to himself.

She sat up and buried her face in her hands. How could she leave him today with so many unanswered questions between them? How could she leave today, period? She would be returning to a lonely house but a good job. Nina was right. That job couldn't keep her warm at night. Nor could it hold her when she needed to be held.

Donna also needed to face the possibility that Isaac might have become used to not having her in his life and would want to keep things that way. He probably liked the sex they'd shared this weekend, but overall, she was more of a bother than she was worth. That thought tore at her heart. She didn't want to believe that, but what else could she think, when he hadn't even asked her to stay an extra day? Not a single one.

A sob was wrenched from her throat. She felt tears wet her hands, but she couldn't help it. She loved Isaac. She had always loved Isaac, even when she truly didn't understand the depth of that love. Sure, she had the career she'd wanted and had worked hard to achieve, but she had been miserable the last three years.

It was all her fault and she doubted she would ever forgive herself. Not able to help herself, she began crying in earnest. One day, another woman would share his heart, have his children, and wear his name.

She wouldn't be the only Mrs. Isaac Elloran. He might even ask that she go back to using her maiden name, Oliver. That made her cry even harder.

Suddenly she was pulled into big strong arms. She didn't have to look up to know who was holding her. His manly scent gave it away and like always, he was comforting her from whatever was breaking her down. Too bad he didn't know that losing him had not only broken her, but it had also left her ruined for anyone else.

"Shh, it's okay, sweetheart. Whatever is bothering you, it's okay," he said, walking across the room with her in his arms to sit down on the loveseat.

"No, it's not okay, Isaac. It's not," she blubbered, knowing he just didn't understand.

He tightened his arms around her while she cried. "Tell me what's wrong so I can try to fix it."

She buried her face in his chest because his words made her cry harder. He shouldn't have to fix it. She was the one who'd broken it. "You can't fix it."

"I used to be able to fix things that were wrong with you, Donna. Please let me try."

She shouldn't tell him anything but couldn't stop herself. The way he had her cuddled in his arms, stroking her back and speaking to her in such a consoling voice...it broke her. She lifted her head to look at him, and the words came pouring out. "I messed up, Isaac. I really messed up."

He lifted a brow. "At work? Did somebody call to tell you that you messed something up at work?"

She studied his features. Did he honestly think that all her tears were about her job? Yes, he would think that, because she'd never given him reason to believe anything was more important to her than her career. Not even him. That made her bury her head in his chest and start crying again.

And he held her, gently stroking her back and telling her that everything was going to be all right. That she was a great employee and if her company didn't realize that, then screw them. She listened to his words and knew more than ever that she had wronged him in the worst possible way. At no time should he have ever thought that anything was more important to her than him.

She lifted her head and after swiping at her tears, she said. "I'm not talking about messing up at work, Isaac. I'm talking about us."

She saw the surprised look in his eyes. "Us?"

"Yes, *us*." Did he think there wasn't an "us" and wondered why she was bringing it up? If so, then too bad. She was bringing it up. She needed to get it off her chest and out of her heart, even if he didn't want to hear it.

At that moment, her pride meant nothing. "I should not have put my job before you. I should have kept my end of the bargain when we agreed to try a long-distance marriage. And I should not have filed for a divorce."

He didn't say anything for a long moment, but just stared at her. Then he asked as if for clarity, "Are you saying you regret doing those things?"

That's exactly what she was trying to say, although it sounded like she was making a bigger mess of things. She nodded. "Yes. I know it's too late for us, but I wanted you to know that. I couldn't leave without telling you."

He pulled her tighter in his arms. "I don't think it's too late for us, Donna."

"You don't?"

"No."

"But–but you didn't say anything about our relationship all weekend," she said.

"Neither did you."

No, she hadn't. "But I thought you just wanted sex, Isaac."

"And why did you think that?"

Now she was the one who was confused. "Why would I think you'd want anything else, after what I did to us?"

He pulled her closer. "There has never been "just sex" with us, Donna."

"Yes, but that was when you loved me."

"And I still love you."

She pushed back to make sure she'd heard him correctly. "You still love me?"

He nodded. "I've never stopped."

"But we're divorced."

"That was your idea, not mine. And if you thought what we were doing was just about sex, why would you let me use you that way?"

She figured she might as well be totally honest. "Because I needed you. Really bad. And I didn't want you to reject me if I told you how I truly felt."

"And how do you feel, Donna?"

Did he really have to ask? "I love you, too."

He stared at her as if he was weighing her answer. "For how long?"

She didn't understand his question. "For how long?"

"Yes. How long will you love me, Donna? Until your career dictates otherwise?"

She drew in a deep breath, knowing she deserved his doubt. "I will love you forever."

She knew he didn't believe her, and it was her fault that he didn't. "You didn't even ask me to stay with you for a few more days."

"You should know why. How many times, when you came to visit me in Boston, did I ask you to stay, practically begging you to extend your time with me? And you'd almost always turn me down. You weren't the only one worried about being rejected, Donna."

She couldn't say anything for a minute and then after swiping her eyes again, she asked, "So, where do we go from here?"

"You tell me, Donna. If I was to ask you to stay a couple more days so we can get to know each other again, would you?"

Not even stopping to consider anything else, she said, "Yes." She rarely took time off work and had accumulated more vacation days than she'd ever need.

He studied her features, as if searching for the truth. She was tempted to look away but didn't. If he was trying to see what he meant to her, then let him look. "If I asked you to stay an additional week, would you?"

She swallowed. He was pushing the envelope, but she didn't care. "Yes."

He nodded slowly. "Then stay an additional week with me, Donna. Let's spend more time together and by the end of the week, we'll know what we want to do."

Chapter Thirteen

"I can't believe you still eat so much," Donna said, grinning over at Isaac.

He chuckled. "And I can't believe you volunteered to cook."

After deciding to stay the week, she had called her office to let them know she was taking the time off and would see them next Tuesday. Then they went back to bed and made love again. It wasn't until their stomachs grumbled that they decided to get up. They had missed lunch and he'd been surprised that Donna had offered to cook dinner.

When they were married, they rarely ate at home and when they did, he did most of the cooking. After his mother died, he'd learned how to cook for survival purposes. His father had put in long hours at the repair shop, sometimes working well into the night, so it was to either learn to cook or starve.

And he had to admit, being Ry's best friend meant that he hung around Witherspoon Café a lot, since Ry helped out his parents after school. And if Ry was in the kitchen, then Isaac was usually in there with him, learning the tricks of the trade. He'd even surprised his dad a time or two with a meal he'd whipped up from scratch.

"I learned to cook because I didn't like going to restaurants by myself," she said, after placing the plate of food in front of him. "I wasn't used to eating alone."

He lifted a brow. "What happened to your girlfriends? Those co-workers you used to hang out with?"

She took her seat across from him and he saw the tightening of her jaw. That had always been a sure-fire sign that what she was about to say annoyed her. "What happened was that I became the odd one out, the woman without a man. Would you believe they actually thought that, since I no longer had a man of my own, I would set my sights on theirs?"

"They actually told you that?"

She picked up her fork and almost stabbed the baked potato with it. "Not at first. But they stopped inviting me over for dinner or shopping or anything. I started to wonder why, so I asked them. At least they were honest about it."

He shook his head as he tasted the meatloaf. They had been her friends, yet they didn't trust her around their husbands. "You're better off without them."

"Yes, I am. And since I didn't go out much, I started watching a lot of cooking shows and decided I liked it."

"Well, this is good. I am impressed." In addition to the meatloaf, she had made Cajun mashed potatoes and gravy, green beans, and cornbread. Everything was delicious.

She smiled. "Thank you, Isaac."

"You are welcome, sweetheart."

Dinner was great and he enjoyed sharing the evening with her. It gave them both a chance to get to know each other again. He told her that although retirement was nice, doing those specials jobs for Kaegan and Reid Lacroix had made him realize just how much he missed working. Reid had approached him about setting up a more modern security system at the blueberry plant, and he was considering it. She told him about the projects she'd been working on, but it seemed to him that she'd lost some of the enthusiasm she used to have when she'd talked about her job.

They had finished dinner when the doorbell sounded. "I'll get that. That's probably Brody." They both knew Brody, since he'd attended school with them.

Brody had returned to the cove last year to take over for his father as Fire Chief Investigator when Brody's father had retired early due to illness. The man had subsequently passed away nine months ago.

At the ice cream social, he and Brody had talked about their mutual love of fishing. When Isaac had mentioned he had an extra fishing rod Brody could have, Brody had said he would drop by one day this week to get it.

The last person Isaac expected to find when he opened the door was Alicia...who immediately threw herself into his arms.

He was just pushing Alicia away when he heard Donna say, "I hope I'm not interrupting anything."

Alicia glared at Donna. "What are you doing here? I thought you had left town earlier today."

Donna crossed her arms over her chest. "Sorry to disappoint you."

Frowning, Isaac turned to Alicia. "What are you doing here, Alicia?"

She smiled up at him. "Don't you remember? You invited me. You told me to come today."

Isaac shook his head. "I told you no such thing."

"You did. Don't claim otherwise because your ex is here. And why are you worried about what she thinks anyway? You're too good for her. You were always too good for her."

Angered beyond reason, Isaac crossed his arms over his chest as well. "But I suppose I'm perfect for you, right?"

She smiled. "Of course."

Isaac dropped his hands. "First of all, I refused to get involved with women who are liars. If they lie about one thing, they will lie about another. I never invited you over here, and you are lying if you said I did. I don't want you. I've never wanted you. The only woman I've ever wanted was my wife—then and now. Not all men are hot for you, Alicia, and I'd appreciate it if you would mark me off your list. Now please leave." He then opened the door.

Alicia turned to Donna. "Isaac did invite me over here. He's only acting that way because he got caught. And he does want me," she said, before strutting out the door.

Isaac slammed it behind her. He couldn't believe this. Could there be any worse timing? Reluctantly, he turned to Donna. "Who do you believe?"

Dropping her hands to her side, she stared at him, as if surprised at his question. "You of course. You have no reason to lie. Besides, you're free to do whatever you want, with whomever you want. But I doubt it would be with Alicia. If nothing else, you have better taste than that."

Isaac nodded. "I most certainly do."

"Besides," Donna said. "She's using an old play from her gamebook. Remember that time she tried to convince me you had told her to meet you beneath the bleachers and then lied to get you there so I would catch the two of you together?"

He nodded, remembering. "Yes."

"She lied then and she's lying now."

"Thanks for believing in me, Donna." He walked over to her and swept her into his arms. "Let's go back to bed."

"I need to load up your dishwasher."

"Later, sweetheart."

She wrapped her arms around his neck, and he kissed her, letting her know how much he loved her. When he finished, she nodded. "Yes, later."

The next day Isaac talked Donna into having lunch with him at the Witherspoon Café. But when they walked in and found Nina and Arnett there, Donna hissed, "I forgot to let Nina know I was staying and it's all your fault, Isaac."

He chuckled. "And why is it all my fault?"

"Because you haven't let me out of bed in days."

"Are you complaining?"

She grinned cheekily. "Nope."

Nina almost screamed when she saw him and Donna. And when Donna told her friend of her decision to stay until the following Monday, Nina winked over at him. Isaac figured that was her way of letting him know she was on his side—at least, in this situation.

Before they got their meal, other friends who'd decided to stay in town a little longer—and who knew where you could always get a delicious meal—joined them. Pretty soon, it was like another reunion. Ry came out from the kitchen to join them and the group spent more than two hours reminiscing about growing up in Catalina Cove.

Kaegan eventually staggered in and Bryce snagged the chair next to him. Isaac looked around. It felt good to be here with people he'd known for years, but more importantly, it felt wonderful to be here again with Donna. She seemed to be having a good time, and he finally felt like he'd be able to relax.

A few hours later, they left the café and walked to his car, holding hands. He was thinking about asking her out on the boat, but the weather was a little too chilly. It was unlikely she'd want to do that.

"Don't you agree, Isaac?" she asked, as he opened the car door for her.

He lifted a brow. "Agree with what?"

"That we need to decorate your house for Christmas. You're probably the only person in Catalina Cove who doesn't have a tree yet."

He grinned. She was right. The people in town went overboard decorating their homes for Christmas. They even decorated their boats—on Christmas Eve. Boats all decked out in Christmas finery would parade around the cove with lights flashing. There was even a prize for the most decorated boat.

"I won't need a tree unless you intend to join me for Christmas."

He watched her features and saw the sparkle shine in her eyes. "I'd love to come back, Isaac. Thanks for asking me."

He leaned down to buckle her seatbelt. Had she honestly thought that he wouldn't ask her? He had spent the three past Christmases without her, and he really didn't want to do it again. "We can pick up a tree and all the decorations now, if you're up to it." He couldn't help reminding her that they'd spent most of the night making love, which was why they'd slept through breakfast.

Last night, they'd also done something they hadn't done in years—they'd sat curled up together on the sofa in front of the fireplace and gone through their yearbook. Seeing all those youthful faces and comparing them with what those adults looked like now, had been fun. Not everyone had improved with age.

But Donna had. It had been wonderful waking up with her this morning. Just knowing she would be spending the next few days with him, and sharing his bed at night, made him feel good all over.

"Does Mr. Dunbar still have his Christmas tree farm?" she asked him.

"Yes, but his son runs things now. People still come from miles around to get a Dunbar Christmas Tree. We better hope they have some left."

Grinning, she lifted a hand with her fingers crossed. "I am hoping."

A few hours later, although the Dunbar Christmas Tree lot was pretty picked over, they still managed to find the perfect one. At least Donna thought it was perfect. Isaac wasn't so sure. He thought it was way too big, but she had already decided where it should be placed in his living room.

On their way back to his place, they stopped at one of the stores in town to purchase some ornaments. Since Isaac didn't have anything, they had to buy practically everything.

Donna had almost forgotten how much fun holidays were in Catalina Cove. Because there were no major department stores in town, most people drove into New Orleans to shop. Ray Sullivan, one of Kaegan Chambray's close friends and the father of those cute twin babies, was working on starting a river taxi service. Like Reid Lacroix had said at the dance Friday night, a taxi service would certainly cut down on road traffic from the cove to New Orleans.

Once they got back to Isaac's place, they decorated the tree together. It had become cold outside, so she had made them some hot apple cider. Later that evening, they were going to meet Nina and Arnett for dinner at a restaurant in New Orleans.

Donna wished the peace and harmony between her and Isaac could last forever.

"How big is the tree at your place this year?" Isaac asked, as they stood side by side, his arm around her shoulders, to admire the tree. It wasn't yet dark outside, but they couldn't resist turning on the Christmas lights anyway.

She glanced over at him. "I don't have a tree." And then, because she figured he might eventually hear about it from Nina—it was a sore spot with her best friend—she added, "I haven't put up a Christmas tree in three years."

He just looked at her, his dark eyes seeing more than she wanted to reveal. "You told me about not looking at Christmas cards, but are you saying that you didn't put up a tree, either?"

She nodded.

He tightened his arms around her, not saying anything. In truth, nothing needed to be said. He knew how much she loved Christmas, and for her not to have had a tree since he'd left... That meant something. The fact that he hadn't had one either. That meant something, too.

Getting the tree had always been a big part of the holidays for them. For them, the holidays didn't officially start until after they'd decorated their home. It had become a ritual for them that the day after Thanksgiving, they would wake up early and head for Christmas tree lot. Neither of them would think of putting up a fake tree.

"You've still got all the decorations we collected over the years, though, right?"

"Of course, I do. They mean everything to me."

And she meant it. Some of the ornaments had been handed down to her from her parents and from his—like the one he'd made especially for her when they'd been seniors in high school, and the ornament his mother had made for him the Christmas before she'd passed away, as well as the one she'd inherited from her father's mother—a crystal snowflake that had been passed down through four generations.

He took a sip of his drink. "This apple cider is really good."

She smiled. "Thanks. That's Nina's grandmother's recipe. I loved her apple cider."

"And I always enjoyed it whenever you made it."

She warmed inside, knowing he remembered her doing that during the holidays. "You were living in the cove last Christmas, right?"

He nodded. "Yes. I had just moved back to town and was living in an apartment. I hadn't decided what I was going to do, but I was just glad to be back home. Some people had heard we'd gotten a divorce, but a lot hadn't. Those who hadn't would ask about you, thinking you were here with me and when they discovered otherwise, I could see the look of regret on their faces."

Donna understood. It had been that same way for her. People in the places they used to frequent would ask about him and she hadn't had the heart, nor the right frame of mine, to tell them they weren't to-gether anymore. As a married couple, they'd been almost inseparable. In a way, that had been the root of the problem. And it was one of the things they needed to talk about.

She eased down on the sofa that faced the tree so she could still look at it. For some reason, seeing all the twinkling lights gave her hope, and a sense that she might be able to find what she'd thought was long gone.

"I think one of the reasons I found so much pleasure in my work, Isaac, was because it was the only time that I had any space from you."

She saw him stiffen and reached out to touch his arm, urging him to sit down on the sofa as well.

"I didn't know you needed space from me, Donna," he said as he sat.

Donna heard the hurt in his tone. She hadn't meant to be hurtful, just truthful. She knew the only way he could understand what she'd been going through at the time was to try to explain it to him. "Just think about it, Isaac. We'd been together since I was seventeen. We were practically inseparable." She smiled. "My parents and your father would say we hung around each other so much. we were beginning to look alike."

He smiled. "They did say that, didn't they?"

"Yes. And after high school, we attended the same college, lived in the same dorm, and then in two years, we moved into our own apartment. We took as many classes we could take together, and during all that time, we never dated anyone else."

He nodded. "I didn't want to date other people. Did you?"

She shook her head. "No. It never crossed my mind. I was too into you."

"You didn't complain," he said, a little accusingly.

"No, I didn't, because I never had a reason to do it. I loved being into you, Isaac."

"What changed, Donna?" he asked in a calm voice, taking one of her hands and holding it tight.

She took a sip of her apple cider. "I changed, Isaac. At some point, I discovered I needed my own identity. We'd become this one being—not Donna and Isaac anymore. I'd nearly forgotten what it felt like being my own person. Everything I did was centered on you or on us. I didn't ever do anything just for me."

Donna knew how selfish she was sounding, but she needed him to understand her. She was all into her feelings now and wanted to share those feelings, no matter how he saw them. If she didn't use this time to be open and honest with him, she'd regret it. She might never have this opportunity again.

"Are you saying you became unhappy being married to me, Donna?"

She held his gaze. "No. I'm saying I lost myself while being married to you, Isaac. I wanted it all, both you and my career. Then I discovered I couldn't have it all. I had to make sacrifices."

"And I became the sacrificial lamb, is that it? You decided that finding yourself meant more to you than loving me?"

His words sounded harsh, insensitive, critical, and even unkind. But in a way, what he said was true. "At the time, I was struggling to survive, Isaac. I needed to know myself and accept myself as a whole person and not just your half."

Donna wasn't sure if she was getting through to him. And she didn't know how else to tell him.

Then he asked her, "And have you done that, Donna? Have you found yourself without me?"

She shook her head. "What I ultimately realized, Isaac, unfortunately too late, was that I could have found myself with you, had I gone about it in the right way."

"And what would you have done different?"

She nibbled on her bottom lip. "First, I would have taken the time to discover that I could have had it all. Both you and the career I wanted. I would have also come to realize that being me didn't mean I had to lose you. I just would have had to work harder to maintain both. I should have realized you were worth the effort. That our marriage was worth the effort."

She paused a moment and then added, "And finally, I would have kept my end of the bargain and put more effort into our compromise. I should have accepted that if anything had to go, it would have had to be my job, not my husband, who'd done nothing but support me. But I didn't do that. I got so caught up in looking good at work that I forgot what was most important to me. And that was you."

He didn't say anything for the longest time. Then releasing her hand, he reached out gently and took hold of her chin. "I wished you'd told me how you felt, Donna. Explained the inner struggles you were going through. I would have—"

"You would have tried even harder to make things work. You already did everything you could, and now I see that it wasn't fair to you."

He stood and pulled her into his arms. "Come on, let's get ready for our dinner in New Orleans. Thanks for sharing that with me. I just want you to know that I love you, Donna, and I believe we can get through this. But you have to believe that, too."

She nodded—she wanted to believe it, more than anything. But there was one other thing she was desperate to know. "Can I ask you something, Isaac?"

He nodded. "You can ask me anything you want."

She tilted her head to see the look in his eyes when he answered her question. "How can you not hate me for destroying what we had?"

Chapter Fourteen

Isaac released a deep breath, knowing they were doing what they needed to do—talk, and get their issues out in the open so they could deal with them. And they also had to deal with their feelings. The hurt and the anger. There was no way they could move forward without dealing with the past.

"I did hate you, Donna. Well, at first, I might have. I couldn't believe you would give up on me, on us, like that. I became bitter and angry. It was Uncle Mark who made me see reason, made me realize I was just as much to blame. I should not have forced us into a stalemate—giving you an ultimatum like that. Uncle Mark felt that once I'd pushed you back against the wall, forcing you into making a choice, it wasn't your fault that you decided to do what you thought was best for you." Isaac paused a minute. "At some point, did you start to hate me, Donna?"

She shook her head. "No, I could never hate you," she said softly. "When I realized you weren't coming back and that I was the one who'd screwed up, I was disappointed with myself. I decided to give you your freedom because I felt I no longer deserved you. I had done the very thing I swore I would never do—let you down. I had gotten caught up in my job and with women who I'd thought were my friends. I realized too late that they'd been jealous all along of what I had with you. And in the end, I lost what was most important to me."

He was glad she'd found out those women hadn't truly been her friends. However, he regretted that it had been such a painful realization for her. "We've talked enough for today. I'm in the mood to do something else before we get ready to go out to dinner."

"What were you thinking of, Isaac?"

"This." And he leaned down and claimed her mouth.

Donna was in the mood for this as well. How had she gone nearly three years without his taste? His heat? His warmth? The very essence of him in her life? They'd been trying to make up for lost time, but she doubted she'd ever get enough of this. Of him.

He wanted her. She knew that. The huge erection pressing against the juncture of her thighs was a dead giveaway, as well as the intensity of his kiss. He devoured her mouth in that way he had that would leave her moaning and hungry for more. In seconds, her entire body was on fire and he was the only person who could put it out.

When he released her mouth, she leaned closer and licked the side of his face, right beneath his ear. He knew exactly what that meant, what she'd just communicated to him. She needed him, now.

He took her mouth again, angling his head to feast greedily. She returned his kiss with a hunger that matched his. There was no way he wouldn't be able to tell she had truly missed this. His mouth on hers. The feel of his throbbing shaft pressing hard against her. Being held in his arms.

His tongue was still working its magic in her mouth, seducing her in ways that only he could. Blood was rushing like crazy through her veins and she could feel herself drowning in the taste and scent of him.

Donna was so absorbed in the kiss that she hadn't realized Isaac had used his fingers to undress her. When he pulled back, her dress fell in a heap at her feet and she was left wearing only a barely-there black thong and bra.

In one smooth tug, he practically ripped off her undies and un-hooked her bra. Immediately his fingers were at her center, stroking her into a sensuous daze.

"I love doing this to you," he leaned forward to whisper. The moist heat from his breath warmed the area beneath her ear.

"And I love you doing this to me, Isaac."

"I need you, Donna," he said, quickly removing his own clothes. "Here. Now. Right underneath the Christmas tree. You will be my Christmas present. No bow, no wrapping paper needed. Just a naked you."

Grabbing one of the huge pillows off the sofa, he tossed it on the floor by the tree before pulling her down on it with him. Then he was there, straddling her, lifting her hips as he thrust hard into her, as if needing to be joined with her right then. Right there.

She was hot, wet, and ready for him, just the way he liked. He continued to thrust into her, and the more she moaned his name, the harder his thrusts came. This was the woman he loved. The woman he needed. "I can't get enough of you," he moaned.

"Good. I don't ever want you to get enough of me."

Their gazes connected. He loved her and would always love her. She screamed his name and he threw his head back as an orgasm struck. Her muscles clamped down on him, pulling everything out of him. Draining everything he had to give. He didn't mind. He wanted her to have it all. He wanted her to take all of him.

She did.

One orgasm led to another. Then another. Finally, he rolled off of her, barely able to catch his breath. "If we don't stop, we're going to be late for dinner," he said, trying to rationalize the situation.

"And?"

He glanced over at her and smiled. Then he rolled back on top of her. "And I guess we'll just have to be late."

"What do you want to do today sweetheart?"

Donna glanced over at Isaac, thinking she loved it when he called her that. It was hard to believe it was Thursday already. They had only three more days to be together. The more time she spent in Catalina Cove, the more she wanted to spend here; especially with Isaac. The good thing was that she would be returning in two weeks to spend Christmas and New Year's with him.

They already had activities lined up for the two weeks she planned to stay. They would be going to the boat parade on Christmas Eve, after getting things ready for their Christmas dinner. It would be the first time they'd ever shared a kitchen and she was looking forward to it.

It had been close to ten in the morning before they got out of bed. He had prepared breakfast and she had helped. Then, over breakfast, he'd brought her up-to-date as to what was happening in Catalina Cove. He'd told her it had finally been revealed who'd gotten Vashti pregnant, back when they were in high school—Reid Lacroix's deceased son, Julius. In the end, things had turned out well. Vashti had her twin daughters and Reid Lacroix was an overindulgent grandfather.

He also explained the situation with Kaegan and Bryce and how they'd gotten back together after ten years apart."

"I'm glad things worked out for everyone," she told him.

"So am I. And by the way, did you know we have another celebrity living in the cove?"

She lifted a brow. "Who?"

"Victoria Madaris. She has a morning talk show on Channel Two in New Orleans. But what really has the locals excited is that she's the niece of Jacob Madaris, who's married to actress Diamond Swain Madaris."

Donna didn't watch television a lot, nor had she been to the movies in a while. But you didn't have to do either to know who Diamond Swain Madaris was. "And everyone is hoping Diamond decides to pay her niece a visit, right?" she said grinning.

"That's what everyone is hoping," he said, smiling. "The guys are at least. The women are hoping to see the uncle, Jacob Madaris, or his friend, actor Sterling Hamilton."

At that moment Donna's phone rang. She recognized the ringtone and knew Isaac did as well—it was her employer. She wondered why someone at the office would be calling her. She had no pressing projects. In fact, she was ahead of schedule, having finished up all her work for the rest of the year.

"Aren't you going to get that?" Isaac finally asked when it rang again.

"Yes." She clicked on the phone. "Donna Elloran."

"Ms. Elloran, this is James Chase. I'm glad I was able to reach you. Your personal assistant said you were out of town."

Yet you called me anyway, she thought. "That's right. I'm in Louisiana."

"How soon can you get back to the office?"

She frowned. "Why? What's wrong?" She watched as Isaac pushed his chair back from the table to go over to the coffee pot and refill his mug. Then he left the kitchen.

"I need you to work with Lionel McAfee on the Hastings' account. They don't like the presentation his team came up with, so I'm hoping you'll be able to fix it and make them happy again."

Lionel McAfee was the man Mr. Chase had promoted over her. Yet he wanted her to ruin her vacation and rush back to take care of Lionel's mess? The man should be competent enough to fix his own problems.

"When can I expect you here?"

Donna wasn't surprised by Mr. Chase's question. After all, whenever he'd called in the past, needing something done, she would come running. Regardless of what she was doing, where she was...or who she was with. She glanced at the door Isaac had walked out of moments ago. He was probably thinking the same thing and expected her to leave and return to Seattle.

She drew in a deep breath. Her job was important to her, but not as important as Isaac. She had lost him before for placing her career before him, and she refused to do it again. There was no way she would not give Isaac the week he'd asked her for.

"Tuesday," she said. And just in case Mr. Chase didn't understand what she meant, she clarified. "I will be returning to the office on Tuesday. I'm presently on vacation."

There was a pause and then Mr. Chase said in a clipped tone, "I understand that you are currently on vacation, Ms. Elloran, but you are needed here."

And the man she loved needed her *here*. *She* needed to be here. She wanted to be here. Today was Thursday, so the earliest she could get to the office would be tomorrow. What possible difference could one day make to her employer? But then, she knew it wouldn't be one day. More than likely, Mr. Chase expected her to work through the weekend, as well. Fat chance!

"I'm sorry, Mr. Chase but I leave here on Monday, so Tuesday is the earliest I can get there. But even then, I don't know how helpful I'll be since I'm scheduled to have some time off over the holidays."

"That's another thing I need to talk to you about. I had to rescind that time off because you'll be needed here, working to get the Hastings' account back on the right footing."

Donna suddenly saw red. She could not believe this. Then again, she really should not be surprised. All she'd ever been to the company was a tool to carry out whatever duties needed to be done, without any regard to her needs. He had rescinded her time off, without caring what she might have had planned? He hadn't even had the courtesy to ask.

With as much respect as she could muster, she said. "Mr. Chase, I wanted that time off for personal reasons."

"I'm sorry but you are needed here. It's more important."

More important to whom? Definitely not to her and Isaac. "I'm sorry you feel that way, because it's not more important to me. So...I quit. I will email my resignation letter as soon as I can. Goodbye."

Donna disconnected the call, feeling suddenly free. She had worked for that company for ten years, and it had finally sunk in that they did not view her as a person, but as someone whose life they could manipulate for their own ends.

Feeling good, feeling *really* good, she left the kitchen to go find Isaac.

Isaac's heart skipped several beats when he heard Donna approach from behind him. He was standing on his patio looking out at the ocean. He knew the routine by now. She would be leaving. He should be used to it, should have even expected it. But for once, he'd hoped she would keep her word and give them this week. He wanted those three more days with her. He had been prepared to see her leave Sunday, but even that would have been hard on him.

"Isaac?"

He turned and met her gaze. Her expression was unreadable but then, he figured his was too. "When do you leave Donna?" he asked her. "Will you stay until tomorrow or are you needed back now?"

"Mr. Chase wants me to come now."

"That figures," he said drily.

"Yes, but I'm not leaving."

His heart suddenly went from missing beats to racing. "You're leaving in the morning?" he asked for clarification.

She shook her head. "No, I'm not leaving then, either. I'm leaving Monday as planned. Unless..."

He swallowed deeply. "Unless what?"

"Unless you invite me to stay longer."

He shoved his hands into the pockets of his jeans. "Can you stay longer, Donna? I thought you were going back to work next week."

She shrugged. "I had planned to do that...when I had a job."

He lifted a dark bow. "What do you mean? Don't you have a job now?"

"No. I quit."

"You quit your job?"

"Yes." She told him of her conversation with Mr. Chase.

"What makes me madder than anything is that the person he wants me to rescue is someone he promoted over me a couple of months ago. Then, when he assumed that my life and what I want to do on my time off wasn't important, well, it was the last straw."

She reached out and took Isaac's hand. "But more than any of those things, I realized that I deserved all the time I could get with you. I'd put my career before you for too long. Losing you because of it will be something I will regret for the rest of my life."

Isaac pulled Donna into his arms and held her tight. She had always been, and would forever be the love of his life, the one person he loved, adored and cherished. "I happen to think you made a good call by not letting them push you around. Screw them. Besides, I have a career opportunity I'd like to present to you."

"You do? What?"

"Become my wife. And trust me, it comes with good benefits and plenty of room for advancement. How does motherhood sound to you?"

He saw tears suddenly appear in her eyes. "Oh, Isaac. You want to re-hire me as Mrs. Isaac Elloran?"

He chuckled. "I most certainly do. So, what do you think?"

She stood up on her tiptoes and wrapped her arms around his neck. "I think that's the best idea ever. I accept your offer, and I look forward to motherhood. You're the best thing to ever happen to me."

"And you for me," he told her.

"Let's call my parents and tell them our good news. They will be happy for us."

"Umm, let's call them in a little while," Isaac said. Smiling, he pulled her into his arms and closed his mouth over hers. He was determined that this time, they would be happy forever. Together.

Epilogue

Isaac and Donna remarried on Christmas Day, in the same church where they'd first exchanged their vows years ago. Nina and Arnett were in attendance; Donna's parents had returned to the cove as well. It was a private ceremony but some of their friends in town had been invited. A small reception was held in the church's dining hall.

Kaegan and Bryce had shared some good news—they'd moved their wedding date up from June to February. Kaegan was definitely happy about that. Vashti and Sawyer were also bursting to share that they had decided on a name for their daughter. She would be named Shelby, after Vashti's aunt.

The night before their wedding, Donna and Isaac had watched the boat parade, and decided that next year, they'd enter the parade with a decorated boat of their own. Donna would move permanently to Catalina Cove the first of the year. She hadn't decided what she was going to do once she got there, but Isaac had told her she really didn't have to do anything at all. She could become a beach bum like him.

They had both decided they were way too young to retire completely and were considering engaging in some sort of business. Isaac had laughed at Donna's suggestion that they open an ice cream shop in town, but when he saw she was deadly serious, he decided to really give it some thought.

"Are you happy, Mrs. Elloran?" Isaac asked his wife that night, as they lay naked in each other arms on a blanket in front of the fireplace.

They had decided to postpone their honeymoon to Paris until the renovations on the upper part of their house were completed in the spring. Besides, there was no place like Paris in the spring.

"I'm extremely happy."

"Good. So am I. I love you, Donna," he whispered against her lips.

"And I love you, too, Isaac." And she knew that now that she had him in her arms again, she would never let him go. He was all she ever wanted and needed.

He was her everything.

Stay tune...

FOLLOW YOUR HEART,

the next Catalina Cove novel, comes out in October 2020!

Sneak peek...

*Turn the page for an excerpt of Brenda Jackson's next novel,
that's coming out in February 2020 and titled,*
THE BENNETTS' WEDDING

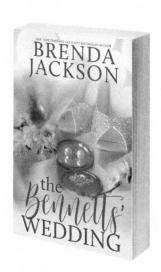

THE BENNETTS' WEDDING

It's been fifteen years and now those Bennett girls are all grown up, finished with college and ready to take on the world in their new careers. Close as ever, Kennedy, Victoria, Monica and Sebrina decide not to return to Georgia, but to move to St. Paul, Minnesota. They have plans to succeed at all of their goals. Falling in love isn't on the agenda.

In THE BENNETTS' WEDDING (February, 2020), Kennedy and Victoria discover when it's your time, you can't hide from love.

• • •

In THE BENNETTS' CHRISTMAS (December, 2020), Monica and Sebrina discover romancing around the holidays are the best!

Kennedy

Today will start out not being such a good day, but don't despair. In the end it will be the best day of your life.

Kennedy Bennett frowned after reading her horoscope in that morning's newspaper. It certainly explained why her morning had gotten off to a bad start. She'd gotten dressed for work only to discover she'd forgotten to pick up from the cleaners the jacket she'd intended to wear today. That meant borrowing one of Sebrina's jackets. Or did the jacket belong to Victoria? It didn't matter since her three house-mates -- Victoria, Monica and Sebrina -- were also her cousins, and were the same size and had no problem sharing.

After getting dressed, she'd pulled out the shoes she intended to wear and noticed a broken heel. To top things off, moments later, a text from her dad broke the news that his best friend, Morgan Viscount, had been in a car accident. Thank goodness he had minor injuries and was fine.

Kennedy could clearly see that her day had definitely gotten off to a bad start. No matter how awful things were going so far, she had to believe today would end well, just like her horoscope predicted.

Her fascination with astrology began a few months ago when she'd hooked up with one of her friends from her teen years, Faith Norwood. There had been a time when Kennedy and Faith, along with Faith's twin sister Grace, had been inseparable. Needless to say, the three of them had always managed to get into trouble while growing up. Faith was now a professor at a university in Nevada, and Grace worked as an accountant in a firm in New York.

The three of them had reunited when Grace and Faith returned to St. Paul for their grandmother's funeral. Grace left to return to New York a couple of days after the services; but Faith had remained in St. Paul for a couple of weeks to help her parents disperse of her grandmother's belongings.

Over lunch Faith had told Kennedy how she'd gotten into astrology and why she believed daily readings of the horoscope was a way to gain a sense of meaning in one's life. She challenged Kennedy to at least try it a few times.

At first Kennedy had indulged for entertainment purposes only. Then when things began happening like her horoscope would predict, it nearly freaked her out. That's when she made it a habit to read her horoscope each morning at the start of her day.

"Aren't you going to be late for work, Kennedy?"

She glanced over at her cousin Sebrina, the only other doctor in the Bennett family, after having followed in their older cousin Rae'jean's footsteps. "No, I'm not late. All the marketing analysts have a meeting today at one. That means that I don't have to go into the office until then. I have a few errands to do this morning, which is good since I need time away from Rivers, even if it's just for a few hours."

Since graduating from college with a Master's degree in marketing, for the last four years she'd worked as an analyst for one of the top marketing firms in St. Paul. Namely, Rivers Marketing and Technological Enterprises. The job paid well, provided good benefits and offered opportunities for advancement...or so she thought. Two weeks ago, she'd gotten overlooked for a junior management position, and it was a promotion she'd worked hard for.

When Kennedy had discovered who'd gotten the job over her, she'd been furious. Larry Matthews had less time with the company than Kennedy, was known to miss deadlines more often than not, and had a bad attendance record. It angered her every time she thought about it. His work record was so bad that people called him "Lazy Larry" behind his back.

"Is that my jacket?"

Sebrina's question pulled Kennedy away from her thoughts. "Yes, it's yours. I forgot to pick mine up from the cleaners and this one works great with my outfit. I hope you don't mind."

Sebrina smiled as she joined Kennedy at the table after pouring a cup of coffee. "Of course, I don't mind. I guess Monica and Victoria have left already."

"Yes, they were leaving when I walked into the kitchen twenty minutes ago."

Kennedy didn't say anything for a moment as she drank her coffee. Although she and her three cousins had gone to separate universities. Monica, Sebrina and Victoria had agreed to move with her to St. Paul after college and become her house-mates. The arrangement was perfect since the four of them had always gotten along.

"I wish you had gotten that promotion, Kennedy. I know how hard you've worked to prove yourself."

Kennedy had worked hard to prove herself. She tried not to let the thought bother her that in a few weeks, Lazy Larry would be her boss. "Thanks for the support Bree. I'm not looking forward to Larry taking over things."

"Have you heard from Charles lately, Kennedy?" Sebrina asked her a few moments later.

Both pain and anger sliced through Kennedy at the mere mention of her ex-fiancé's name. "No, and after my last conversation with him, I doubt that I will again."

"What happened? Did you let the old you come out again? The one with the ability to slice a man in two with just your look?"

Kennedy shrugged. She was known, depending who she was dealing with and when, to let her stubborn and rebellious side not only come out but take over. It was something her father and his wife Taye, had warned her about on numerous occasions. She had mellowed somewhat over the years, trying to master the art of self-discipline and keeping her cool. However, as far as she was concerned, no one had deserved a Kennedy Bennett no-hold-barred unleashing than Charles. He'd honestly thought she would take him back after what he'd done.

Like he could be forgiven after being caught in bed with another woman. Fat chance!

It had been hard the past five months, but she'd survived. The daily readings of her horoscope had helped to provide her with a better understanding of some of the crap she was going through and how to deal with it. A protective shield now covered her heart and she couldn't see it getting removed any time soon. Since then she'd tried getting back into dating but discovered she didn't have time for any man's BS. Some saw women as a sex object and nothing more, and she had no intention of being hurt by another man.

One of the reasons she hadn't dated much in college was because she was someone who refused to be manipulated or controlled. Most guys hadn't liked a defiant woman and she was no man's "yes" girl. She'd honestly thought Charles was different. More than once he'd stated that he liked her feisty attitude and no-tolerance BS position. And with them being able to get along as well as they had, she'd truly believed he'd been the one she felt safe in giving her heart to. She would not have agreed to marry him if she hadn't thought so.

"Why are you asking about Charles, Bree?" Kennedy wondered if Charles had told anyone of her threat to cut off his most precious his body part if he contacted her again.

"Because the two of you were to have gotten married in six weeks. I spoke to your dad yesterday, and I could tell he's worried about you."

Her father, Michael Bennett, would always worry about her. For years it had been just the two of them after her mother passed away when Kennedy was seven. She hadn't made things easy for her father; especially when she'd turned thirteen. She'd started getting into all kinds of trouble and hanging with the wrong crowd at school. She would be the first to admit she had truly earned the title of hellion.

Her rebellious teen years were the reason behind her father's decision to move from St. Paul to Atlanta to be around family. She had thrown all kinds of temper tantrums about the move, but he'd ignored every last one of them.

In the end, she would admit moving to Atlanta had been the best for the both of them. For her it had been meeting numerous cousins she hadn't known. Now she considered Sebrina, Monica and Victoria not only her favorite cousins but also her best friends. For her father, moving to Atlanta meant falling in love again and marrying Taye.

Bree was right. Her wedding day would have been six weeks from now. She was glad she had found out the truth about Charles before the wedding and not after. "I'll call Dad later today to assure him again that I'm doing fine," she said.

"That might be a good idea. I think he still blames himself for introducing you to Charles."

Like her father, Charles was a pilot for a private corporation in Atlanta. She knew the only reason her dad had introduced them was because he had truly liked the guy. She and Charles had hit it off and things had gotten serious between them. He lived in Atlanta and hadn't had a problem with long-distance dating and neither had she. He had flights into St. Paul all the time and they managed to see each other often.

After dating seriously for eight months, he'd asked her to marry him. Since she'd always wanted to be as June bride, they were to marry in June, and he would relocate with his company to their St. Paul's office. They had talked about buying a home in one of the newer housing communities on the outskirts of town.

One day she'd made an unexpected trip to Atlanta. With the house key Charles had given her, she had let herself into his home, thinking she would surprise him. The surprise had been on her instead. She would also admit it had been on Larry and some flight attendant he'd met that day.

The scene that followed hadn't been pretty. Charles had discovered to what degree of a hellion she could be when provoked, and the woman in his bed had no choice but to flee into the night, practically naked.

Kennedy had told her father countless times it hadn't been his fault for introducing them, and she didn't blame him for anything. He'd been fooled by Charles as much as she had. "I told Dad that he shouldn't think that way, and I'll be sure to tell him so again when I talk to him."

She checked her watch. "I have an appointment at the bank this morning for an auto loan. I'm finally getting a new car."

"About time," Sebrina said smiling.

"Leave 'Faithful Bessie' alone," she said grinning. "She and I have been through a lot together."

"And it shows," Sebrina said, trying to contain her laughter.

Kennedy's car had been a birthday gift from her father when she'd turned sixteen and had been brand, spanking new twelve years ago. When her father had handed her the keys, he'd told her if she was good to her car then it would be good to her.

She had been good to her car and 'Faithful Bessie' hadn't let her down through high school, four years of college or the move to St. Paul. Lately, however, the maintenance was getting costly, and she knew she was doing 'Faithful Bessie' a disservice by still expecting top performance. It was time for the old girl to retire.

A short while later when Kennedy left home for her appointment at the bank, she noticed she had a flat tire. As she pulled her phone from her purse to call the emergency road service company to come and change it, she shook her head, hoping this would be the last of her mishaps for today.

It was a beautiful spring day in April, and she hoped whatever good was to happen for her today would hurry up and occur.

• • •

Haddison Bracen Wolf stared across the room at the two men. After eleven years of working as an FBI agent, with seven of those years undercover as Addison Bracey, he was glad for the decision he'd made to make this his last assignment. Otherwise, he would be tempted to blow his cover and cross the room and beat the hell out of Andy Rydell and Vince Sherwin.

Both were the scum of the earth and a part of him regretted the role he'd played for the past three months in getting them to think he was just as dirty and ruthless as they were. The only saving grace was that it wouldn't be long before they were behind bars where they rightly belonged.

In the meantime, he had to stay focused and keep them from getting into serious trouble. They'd laid low for a few weeks, but he could tell they were getting restless. That wasn't good because the FBI was about to wrap things up with the crime ring these two were a part of. To help fund the mob's operation, which included domestic terrorist activities, several banks had been robbed.

The next robbery was scheduled in three weeks. An FBI sting operation was set up for that bank robbery. Things should have been wrapped up weeks ago, but an informant's tip had notified the FBI of a key player in the crime ring that the Bureau hadn't known about. It was vital to find out just who the man was.

Bracey had been disgusted at the names he'd turned in to the Bureau so far. Men highly regarded not only in their communities but on a national scale. But he wasn't surprised. He'd learned from years of working undercover that nobody was as they seemed.

Part of Bracey's job was to befriend Andy and Vince for information. Getting on Andy's good side had been easy enough, but he couldn't say the same for Vince. The man didn't trust him for some reason and was determined to be a thorn in Bracey's side or even more pointedly, a prick in his dick. Vince had put up the most resistance when the Big-Man had told them Bracey would be joining their gang.

"I think we need to rob a bank today."

Bracey's attention was pulled away from his thoughts and back to the pair. "Why?" he asked nonchalantly of Andy. "Our next robbery isn't for another couple of weeks. We have orders from the Big-Man to hang low until then."

"I'm bored. Besides, I got word from someone I can trust that this particular bank will be an easy job."

Honesty? In this business was there really someone Andy thought he could trust? Bracey knew for certain that although Vince had been Andy's partner-in-crime for years, he couldn't be trusted either. Through an informant, Bracey had gotten word that a disc with the names of some of the mob's key players had been hidden somewhere in this house. With the clues provided to him, Bracey had found the disc and had transmitted the names to the Bureau.

Everything had to be timed perfectly and he was hoping nothing went wrong. The stage was set for the Feds to catch them red-handed at the next bank robbery, exactly two weeks from now. When they left the bank assuming they'd mastered another successful heist, both federal agents and the local police, would be waiting to apprehend them.

"We should stay put, Andy," Bracey said, knowing an impromptu bank robbery was definitely a bad idea and could mess up planning.

"Nobody asked you, Bracey, and I agree with Andy. We need to hit a bank without the mob's approval. Then we won't have to turn anything over to those bastards. We can keep everything for ourselves."

Bracey took a sip of his whiskey. He hated the stuff, especially so early in the morning and most of the time he only pretended to drink it as part of his tough guy façade. "You can't betray them. That's death waiting to happen."

"I don't care," Andy snapped.

"And neither do I," Vince echoed. "And like I've been telling you, Andy, you don't have to let the Big-Man treat you like a child who meekly follows his orders. I say let's do it."

Bracey didn't say anything because he knew Vince was goading Andy to make crazy decisions. Why? What was in it for Vince other than money? Both were hard criminals with rap sheets a mile long. Andy was more in control of himself, although he usually didn't think things through before acting. Vince was definitely bad news. Haddison knew his history. The man was a cold-blooded killer and the Bureau wanted to lock him up for good. He was on their most wanted list and had eluded law enforcement for years. Not only was he a loose cannon but a threat to those around him. The Bureau was uneasy about Vince being in this gang because the man could be so unpredictable in the worst sort of way. He had the ability to negatively influence people. Already Haddison could see how he'd begun manipulating Andy.

"I agree. Let's do it," Andy said.

When the room got quiet, Bracey said, "Sounds like you two have made up your minds about it."

"We have," Vince said with a sinister grin. "Now the question is, old man, are you with us?"

They thought of him as an old man since he was thirty-eight to their twenty-five. Most days he felt the thirteen-year difference when dealing with them. They took chances most wouldn't think of taking. The thought of getting caught and serving time again didn't seem to faze them. "What the two of you plan to do is crazy."

"I don't give a damn what you think about it," Vince said. "My question is are you with us or not? Or will you snitch to the Big-Man?"

Andy shook his head. "Bracey won't snitch," he told Vince. He then looked at Bracey. "I've heard you got a good cut from your last job with that cartel out in Vegas. Although some people got caught, and that cartel toppled over, you and a couple of others got away with some of the stash."

Bracey didn't say anything. Andy had heard just what the Bureau had wanted him to hear. They'd carefully built on his reputation from his last assignment. He was surprised no one had ever become suspicious that with each job he never got caught. He would reappear a year or so later as the same person, and thanks to the FBI, with an even more disreputable and dangerous past that could be traced if necessary.

There had been that one time four years ago, when during an assignment, Bracey's duplicity had been uncovered. That's when he had infiltrated the East Coast Connection, an organized crime syndicate that had set its sights on Vegas; specifically, the Grand MD Hotel owned by Lee Madaris and DeAngelo Di Meglio.

Carly, who'd been Lee Madaris' fiancé at the time, was kidnapped. Bracey's identity had gotten compromised when he'd helped her escape from her captor. The FBI had quickly reworked the narrative to make it seem that it was someone else and not Bracey who'd been the FBI's mole.

"You think you know so damn much about me and my business," Bracey finally said, snapping at Andy.

The man only laughed. "Hey, I heard you would turn on your own mother if the price was right."

"Whatever," he said, knowing he was giving them the impression that he would.

"Look, Bracey," Andy said in a coaxing tone. "You were able to stash some money away off that Vegas job a few years back, and all we want to do is the same. If the shit ever hit the fan, the Big-Man will only think of himself. We will be on our own."

"So, are you in with us?" Vince asked, eyeing him crossly.

Bracey waited a beat and then another, before saying, "Yeah, I'm in."

"And I think we should do it today and not wait until night," Vince then said grinning.

Broad daylight. That wasn't Andy and Vince's normal mode of operation. Not good. That meant people could be in harm's way. He needed to alert the Bureau with details the first chance he got. "Why?"

"This particular bank is five hours away in St. Paul. That way the Big-Man won't link us to the hit when the bank robbery makes the news. Besides that, they're used to us working at night, not in the day time. We're covered on all fronts. There's no way they'll suspect us."

"Are you crazy, man?" Bracey asked, knowing he had to talk them out of such an insane idea. "There will be cameras all over the place. There's no way we won't be identified."

"I'll take care of the cameras as always, and we'll be wearing ski masks," Vince said frowning, obviously not liking Bracey's push back.

Bracey shook his head again. "It still will be too risky. If we knock off a bank during business hours people will be inside."

Andy shrugged his shoulders. "Nobody will get hurt if they do what they are told."

"And what if they don't?" Bracey asked. "I don't particularly feel like killing anybody today," he said with coldness in his voice, as if taking another person's life meant nothing to him other than an inconvenience.

Vince chuckled. "Speak for yourself because I don't mind killing anyone. Let me go at it."

Bracey reached for the coffee pot sitting on the table and poured some into his cup. He then took the plastic stick and stirred it up a bit, giving the impression he was considering the words both men had spoken. Then he looked over at them. "Hitting a bank in broad daylight is a game changer. Count me out. Too risky," he said, narrowing his gaze at them. "I don't like it when things get messy for no reason. I still got a price on my head with the Feds. They have an old score to settle with me and will never take me in alive." He knew Andy and Vince assumed he was referring to the rumor that he'd killed a couple of federal agents in the past.

Bracey knew they wouldn't count him out. If the Big Man did suspect them, they couldn't risk him throwing them under the bus. And even if they entertained the idea of getting rid of him, they wouldn't risk doing that either. He hadn't just popped up on their doorstep one day without a purpose. The Big Man had sent him. That meant if any craziness happened, there would be a price to pay and Vince and Andy knew it. If you ever got caught betraying the boss, you wouldn't live to tell about it. He pushed the thought to the back of his mind that in essence, he was doing that very thing.

"No one gets killed as long as they do what they are told. Agreed?" Andy asked in an agitated voice.

"Agreed," Vince said quickly. Too quickly for Bracey's peace of mind.

Bracey eyed the two men for a while before finally saying, "Agreed."

A broad smile covered Andy's face. "All right, then," he said moving to the table where Bracey sat. "Here's the plan."

Vince came over to the table as well. As Bracey listened to the two men, he knew he had to notify the Bureau immediately. He had a bad feeling about how things would go down. A very bad feeling.

Made in the USA
Coppell, TX
22 October 2020